THE QUETZAL AND THE CROSS

THE LAST MAYAN PRINCE

CONRAD SAMAYOA

Order this book online at www.trafford.com
or email orders@trafford.com

Most Trafford titles are also available at major online book retailers.

Printed in the United States of America.

ISBN: 978-1-4669-4362-9 (sc)
ISBN: 978-1-4669-4364-3 (hc)
ISBN: 978-1-4669-4363-6 (e)

Library of Congress Control Number: 2012911029

Trafford rev. 08/30/2012

 www.trafford.com

North America & international
toll-free: 1 888 232 4444 (USA & Canada)
phone: 250 383 6864 ♦ fax: 812 355 4082

K'iché Cast of Characters

TECÚN UMÁN	also mentioned as Ahau Galel, Tekún, Nima Rajpop Achij, Great Captain General Tecúm, grandson of the K'iche king Don K'iqab, TECÚN UMÁM
IXCHEL	Tecún's fiancée
YUM KAAX IK	Chancellor of the K'iche kingdom.
KAKUPATAK	War chief, mentor of Tecún, formerly adjutant to King Don K'iqab
CHILAM KINICH	Captain, imperial guard
IXMUCANE	Ixchel's mom
K'ETZALIN	Ixchel's sister
AH PUCH KISIN	Priest supreme
IXPIYACOC	Tecún's friend, adjutant to Kakupatak
VUKUB	Tecún's friend, also his adjutant
ACAJAL	K'akchiquel chieftain
XAHIL	Tz'utujil chieftain

Spaniards Cast of Characters

PEDRO DE ALVARADO Y CONTRERAS	Conqueror of Maya kingdoms, fought against Tecún
HÉRNÁN CORTÉS	Conqueror of México, viceroy of New Spain (México), Alvarado's superior
CRISTOBAL OLID	Captain, Alvarado's adjutant
PEDRO PORTOCARRERO	Captain, Alvarado's adjutant
JUAN GODINEZ	Catholic priest, member of Alvarado's expedition
JUAN DIAZ	Catholic Priest, member of Alvarado's expedition
JUAN ARGUETA	Sargent, Alvarado's savior
DIEGO GÓMEZ DE ALVARADO	Pedro de Alvarado's father
MEXIA SANDOVAL	Pedro de Alvarado's mother

Deites

AH MUN, GOD OF MAIZE

AH MUZENCAB, GOD OF BEES

AH PUKUB, GOD OF DEATH

AWILIX, PATRON GODDESS

AKNA, GOD OF FERTILITY, OUR MOTHER

AHAU, LORD OR KING

BALAM-JAGUAR GOD; also used as sorcerer, *brujo* and *shaman*

BULUC CHABTAN, WAR GOD

CACOCH, GOD CREATOR

CHAAK, RAIN GOD

HUN HUNAPÚ, FATHER OF THE MAYA HEROES IXPIYACOC AND VUKUB

IXBALANQUÉ, JAGUAR/SUN

JAKAWITZ, MOTHER GODDESS

NAHUAL, PROTECTOR/GUARDIAN ANGEL

Q'UQ'MATZ or K'UQ'MATZ PATRON OF THE FOUR ROYAL HOUSES OF THE K'ICHE EMPIRE

QUETZALCOATL, WHITE-FEATHERED SERPENT

TEPEU, THE MAKER/CREATOR

TONATIUH, THE SUN (SOL)

TOJIL sometimes called TOHIL—JAGUAR GOD.

VUCUB CAQUIX, BIRD DEMON

XIBALBÁ, RULER OF UNDERWORLD OR HELL

Important Dates and Recordings

AUGUST 11, 3134 (1500 EUROPEAN CALENDAR), BIRTH OF AHAU GALEL OR TECÚN UMÁN (UMÁM)

1488, BIRTH OF PEDRO DE ALVARADO Y CONTRERAS

T'ZOLKIN, SHORT MAYA CALENDAR

HAAB, LONG MAYA CALENDAR

VENUS, MORNING AND NIGHT STAR, RELATED TO UNNATURAL EVENTS,

DISASTERS OR WAR

VENUS CYCLES, FIFTY-TWO WEEKS IN THE HAAB (LONG MAYA CALENDAR)

MAYA PREDICTIONS FOR 6885 YEARS (APPROXIMATELY 2012 AND BEYOND)

NOCHE TRISTE (SAD NIGHT JUNE 30, 1520 to JULY 1, 1520 (TENOCHTITLÁN)

Maya Kingdoms

K'ICHE Also referred as Kek'chi, Quiché
K'akchiquel Also named Cakchiquel, Cachiquel
Tz'utujils Also referred as Zutujils.
The three groups spoke the dialect QATZIJOB'AL,
known popularly as Kekchi, Quiché or K'iche

Cities and Places

K'UMARKAJ Capital of the K'iche kingdom, a.k.a. Gumaarkaj

IXIMCHÉ Capital of the K'akchiquel kingdom.

CHUITINAMIT, Capital Tz'utujil Empire

TENOCHTITLÁN Capital of the Aztec empire, later renamed New Spain

VERA CRUZ Old Spanish settlement of Villa Rica, renamed

Vera—Cruz or presently Veracruz, México

BADAJÓZ Province of Badajóz, Spain; Alvarado's birthplace

LABADEE Also known as Española or Hispaniola, later a French possession, now part of Haiti. Modern day Labadie.

Only The Sky Alone Is There

ONLY THE SEA ALONE IS POOLED UNDER ALL THE SKY; THERE IS

NOTHING WHATEVER GATHERED TOGETHER; WHATEVER MIGHT BE IS

SIMPLY NOT THERE: ONLY MURMURS, RIPPLES IN THE DARK, IN THE NIGHT.

WITHIN SHADOWED WATERS RESIDED A GOD, SOVEREIGN PLUMED

SERPENT, ENCLOSED IN BLUE-GREEN QUETZAL FEATHERS, THE CELESTIAL GOD, HEART OF THE SKY, ALSO CALLED HURRICANE DESCENDED AND JOINED HIM.

From the Maya-K'iche sacred book: Popol Vuh

Chapter 1

Thousands of miles away across the immense Atlantic Ocean, in the highlands of northern Mesoamerica, now Guatemala, still unknown to the Europeans, existed an imposing city called K'umarkaj, a large metropolis, capital of the K'iche Empire, settled by the Quichés—K'iche, the last descendants of the Maya.

The city was laid out around a massive central plaza, with the temple of Tojil the jaguar-god, patron of the city—facing west. The temple of the patron goddess Awilix was facing north. The temple of Jacawitz, a mother deity, was facing south. The most impressive structure oriented to the east was consecrated to K'uq'matz, the white-feathered serpent god, sponsor of the four royal houses of the kingdom. Each house ruled the realm for five years. The temple was built in such a manner that the morning light illuminated the main altar, lending an ethereal atmosphere to it. Inside, in the narthex, a huge statue of Quetzalcoatl greeted the supplicants. This colossal temple also housed the council hall, a large structure where all important discussions of the kingdom took place, where all the crucial decisions were made and approved.

All the temples were built of large blocks made of gray stone, with sumptuous gardens and paths for the faithful to walk and meditate. Hundreds of varieties of flowers adorned the intricate mazes, with the orchids specially lending a multicolored tapestry of white, purple and yellow hues mingled with lazy long curved ferns and complemented with fragrant pines and gurgling fountains.

Four large ball courts were scattered through the city. The Maya were avid ball players, and the seasonal games were attended by thousands of spectators each year. The courts were rectangular structures with a hoop at each end suspended from a wooden pole. The players could move the ball, made of a soft rubbery substance called *copal* using all parts of their body but their hands and try to pass it through the hoop to score points. The metropolis had a population of close to two hundred thousand dwellers.

Hundreds of people were moving in the streets bound for the central court. The din of the four marimbas, one on each cardinal point of the town, along with the haunting notes of the *chirimillas (a reed flute)* and the monotonous beat of the *tuns* (drums), was deafening. The music was like a continuous loop—as soon one ensemble ended, another group immediately took over. The air was filled with music and happiness.

K'umarkaj was absorbed in two celebrations: the annual festival in honor of Ah Pun, the god of maize and the other, a most solemn and joyous affair, for the birth of a prince to the royal house of Tekún. The augurs had prophesied that this child would grow to fulfill his sacred destiny as leader of his nation. His *nahual* (protector) was the quetzal, a small bird of breathtaking beauty, with iridescent green feathers and a deep crimson chest. His tail was long and curved with a span of almost four feet. The quetzal was revered as a symbol of freedom. The Maya lore acknowledged that this gorgeous bird could not live in captivity. The legend further stated that this winged creature was the reincarnation of Quetzalcoatl, the white-feathered serpent, creator and protector of the four royal houses of the Maya-K'iche kingdom.

The astrologers had predicted that these two events would coincide with the alignment of Venus—the morning star—and the sun, an event anticipated by the Maya people for many generations.

"Ah Pun, our divine maize-god the supreme priest invoked, "we humbly pay you homage, you have come to life in the form of our recently born prince Ahau Galel, from the noble house of Tekún, grandson of the great king Don K'iqab." He continued, "We accept this blessed gift with gratitude and joy. May Awilix, our patron goddess, protect and guide his life." The priest said, "Oh, great spirit keep our crops bountiful, make our women more fertile." Then, with great reverence and utmost care, the priest took the baby in his powerful arms and presented the naked infant, raising him to the heavens from atop the rostrum of the temple of K'uq'matz to the throngs of people congregated around the perimeter of the temple. The delirious multitude, upon seeing the child, started shouting, "Ahau, Ahau, Ahau," many shedding tears of joy. His royal house was well liked by the masses. The people had expected this birth for many centuries. Finally the wait was over. The kingdom had an heir, Prince Ahau Galel, Prince Tecún Umán.

The birth occurred on August 11, 3114, of the long Maya calendar, the year of the Lord 1500 in the European calendar. The celebrations continued for three full days, with free food, beverages, and desserts for all the attendees. It was a wonderful occasion. After the ceremony and a final blessing, the multitude dispersed. Some took for the ball parks; others marched toward the margins of the Olintepeque River where most of them were camping.

The kingdom was enjoying an unprecedented advance in astronomy; the astronomers had plotted the path of Venus and other celestial bodies for the next 6885 Venus cycles, each cycle consisting of fifty-two weeks and five additional days considered unimportant. These computations were used as a guide for planting the corn, the main staple of their diet. The priests were, beside astronomy, well versed in medicine, as advanced as to be able to perform cranial trepanations. The use of zero in their calculations was widely employed. Their builders used precious woods for the decoration and support of the buildings. The streets were paved with a special material of charcoal-fired lime, white in color. Some streets were as wide as ninety feet.

Most people were farmers, called *kajols*, or serfs that enjoyed freedom and were owners of their lands. The upper class was composed of the *kaweks* (merchants) with the *ajaws* (nobility or ruling class) in charge of the government and defense. The house of Tekún was one of the oldest and most respected in the realm.

Tecún-Ahau Galel grew up in privilege and was groomed to become the next ruler of the kingdom. His life was devoted at learning the graphic symbols of the Maya, complemented with instruction in music and training in martial arts, as was mandatory and expected for a royal prince.

The years transformed him into a strapping youth with a handsome face with deep, dark, penetrating eyes, like coal, a short slightly aquiline nose, and a determined mouth. His face was framed by long lustrous black hair, enhanced by a smooth bronzed skin and powerful muscles. He had a serious demeanor but could crack a joke with his friends or mingle with ease among the lower classes. Tecún became a deadly shot with the *honda*, a slingshot that could hurtle *bodoques* (rounded, hardened clay pellet) to more than three hundred feet.

He was quick witted and had excelled in the art of hunting with bow and arrows. He was also outstanding with the *lanza* (spear) and the *mazo* (a club studded with shards of a black rock called obsidian, hard as diamonds).

His best friends were Ixpiyacoc and Vukub with whom he associated quite frequently, attending multiple activities, mainly the ball games in one of the four courts of the city. They also regularly hunted deer and other animals together. His father and grandfather had died in one of the many battles against the K'akchiquels and Tz'utujils, their perennial enemies. He could not remember much of his father since he died when Ahau was still young; his grandfather, Don K'iqab raised him with the help of his mother, who was Don K'iqab's daughter. Kakupatak, one of his grandfather's disciples, became his mentor and best friend; Tecún visited his house quite frequently, and with time, Kakupatak became a father figure. Many times Tecún called him *tata* (father). Sometimes he called him Uncle Kaku.

In company of his mentor and his friends Ixpiyacoc and Vukub, Tecún explored the margins of the river hundreds of times; he became intimately familiar with the forests and the animal tracks. Ahau Galel attended some of the religious services and was well versed in religion without being an ascetic.

Chapter 2

adajóz, in the province of Extremadura, in the kingdom of Spain, was an impoverished land, hot, the dusty plains cooled off by a large river that crossed the town; the inhabitants made their living with hard work and enormous sacrifices.

The house of Don Diego Gómez de Alvarado and his second wife, Mexia de Sandoval, was a humble abode, barely big enough to accommodate the many children of Don Diego and Mexia. Don Diego, after being a commander of the garrison of Lobón, official instructor to Enrique IV of Castile and *grado trece* (grade thirteen), a short grade before grand master of the Order of Santiago, saw his fortune plummet, finding himself almost destitute, leasing a small farm, surviving with the meager income brought in from the harvesting of olives and other seasonal crops. His last son, named Pedro de Alvarado y Contreras, was recently born. *Another mouth to feed,* Don Diego thought somberly. Pedro inherited his mother's white skin and deep cerulean eyes. His father's blond hair complemented his handsome face.

Pedro de Alvarado's early life was a hard one, with lots of manual labor from morning until dusk. Most days, after work, Pedro, together with his older brothers and his cousins Rodrigo and Hernando Sosa, went to the margins of the river to play, explore the nearby sites, and walk in the soft sand. The kids soon learned to swim and with time and age became accomplished Tritons. They were a permanent presence in the banks of the river, whose center carried strong undercurrents, with treacherous spots. The turbulent waters transported trunks of uprooted trees, garbage, sometimes corpses of unwary swimmers caught in the powerful streams where they had drowned.

As the years passed, Pedro de Alvarado turned into a handsome youngster with a long golden mane of hair and those intense metallic blue eyes. Pedro and his brothers and cousin Rodrigo constantly played as pirates, sometimes as soldiers of the king, pretending to have battles against the Moors recently expelled from the new nation of Spain after they were defeated by the Catholic king and queen of Aragón and Castile at Granada.

The minds of Pedro and his family were filled with the tales of untold riches coming from the New World recently discovered by Christopher Columbus in 1492. They were led to believe that gold was found in the open lands, ready to be picked by anyone brave enough to sail to these fabled lands.

With times becoming harder and harder, his father had become almost an alcoholic, a recluse, who constantly abused his wife and his children, forever lamenting and blaming them for his fall from grace. For reasons unknown, Don Diego was banned from the court of Castile and lost his place in the Order of Santiago, neglected the religious and literary education of his boys, but sometimes, almost as an afterthought, instructed his children in the use of sword, pike, and knife. Their mother, Mexia, continued to be a devout Catholic and attended mass whenever she could convince her husband to bring her to church. Don Diego always complained of the ungodly hour of the mass, around five in the morning, commenting that he could not understand the babblings of the priest, in Latin. Pedro's mom was a sweet woman, beautiful, young and inexperienced, with poor literary education as was the custom in those times. Nevertheless, she insisted that Pedro, her youngest, attend mass and help the cleric during the service. The priest, sometimes when not drunk, gave Pedro few loaves of bread, some olives, olive oil, and other assorted items. Pedro complained to his mother that the churchman stank of wine, garlic, and old sweat, with his garments soiled with stains of wine. Pedro always wondered how the priest could afford to buy food, let alone wine, but somehow, the cleric always had provisions; later on, Pedro would learn that all these food and wine were given to the priest as alms by the people who could barely feed themselves. He was enraged at this blasphemy—taking bread from the downtrodden.

Mexia had a brother, Alejandro, a carpenter that had moved to Cádiz, a seaport in the Mediterranean from where most of the ships sailing to the New World departed. His mother had told Pedro that Alejandro had offered for them in more than one occasion, to go and live with him and Sara, his wife, in Cádiz, but he had refused, and the older brothers did the same because they were afraid for their mother's safety. In lieu, Alejandro sent, on and off, some money to help alleviate the penurious situation of his sister's family.

The tenuous relationship of Pedro with the priest came to a crashing end one morning when Pedro, by accident, spilled some of the wine recently consecrated; that mistake sent the cleric into a fit of rage, which he vented as soon as the mass was concluded by flogging and verbally abusing Pedro, who abandoned the church in a rush after the punishment to never return despite the constant supplications of his mother.

The cleric had been brutal with the whip, hitting Pedro countless times; each occasion the leather struck his back, the cleric urged Pedro to repent, addressing him in Latin, a language Pedro did not understand, which incensed the cleric even more until he tired of hitting his victim. The face of the minister was red, almost purplish, covered in sweat, his body releasing a ripe odor for lack of a bath, his garments soiled with remnants of food and old wine. During the whipping Pedro did not utter a word, did not shed a tear; he took the flogging with stoicism, in silence. When he finally saw himself free, he stood up, gathered a glob of spittle in his mouth and spit it in the face of the cleric, shouting, "There is no God. God does not exist, If God existed, he will not allow people like you to take advantage of the poor souls, to take their hard-earned coins and spend them buying wine to get drunk. You are a disgrace to the church."

When Pedro got home and told his dad about the incident, his father beat him again for his disrespect of the reverend, yelling at Pedro, telling him that he would never amount to much in life. Alvarado flinched every time the fusta—*whip* struck, but he never cried. His mother and brothers, despite their best intentions, did not intervene. Once his father finished the punishment, he sent Pedro to the stable where he slept with the horses. During the night, he clung to a small mutt, a dog that had been his playmate since he was a little boy. His eyes were cold, hard, and immutable. Early the following morning, his brothers and cousin washed the wounds left by the whip, applying some salve to help with the burning and itch.

Days later, Pedro was sitting by the banks of the river, tracing crosses in the soft sand and rapidly erasing them, his vacant eyes lost somewhere in the horizon, not willing to talk. He was bitterly recollecting the unjustified *castigo* (punishment) he got from the priest and later in the hands of his father.

The river had become his refuge, his playground, the stage where he could indulge his fantasies and live vicariously. Life continued. The days became longer, and it became harder and harder to tolerate the abuses of his dad. His only escape was the river.

Alvarado was afraid that one of these days his father, in one of his fits, would harm his mother, even kill her, but there was nothing he could do, at least for the time being. He kept devising in his mind ways to escape with his mother and bring her to Cádiz, where they could all live happy with Alejandro and Sara, but he was still too young and naive.

One afternoon, while the brothers and their cousin were playing in the river, Pedro's oldest brother, Gonzalo, shouted, "There is a black bag in the middle of the river, it looks heavy. Maybe it belonged to a soldier that drowned and could be filled with gold and precious jewels." But he did not attempt to retrieve the bag. Pedro, without hesitation, went into the water and with powerful strokes reached the bag. To his great amazement, the bundle contained a huge black dog desperately fighting to stay afloat. With great care, Pedro grabbed the bag and with great tenderness spoke to the dog in his softest voice, murmuring, "Don't worry, I will save you." With great determination, he held the dog by the neck, not knowing if the animal would bite him, and carried the soaked dog to the riverbank. Once Pedro reached the beach, his surprise was great when he realized the rescued animal was a bitch and she was pregnant!

Alvarado immediately adopted the animal, caring for her with great dedication and love, feeding her the few scraps of food he could rescue from his home, until finally one day, the tramp delivered six gorgeous puppies, one of them black with liquid yellow eyes. After the critters were weaned, Pedro kept the black one for himself. Another went to his cousin Rodrigo. The rest were given or sold to homes where Pedro knew the puppies would be well tended for. Pedro had named the rescued dog Alma Del Rio (Soul of the River) since she was salved from the waters. Two of Alma del Rio's sons would become Valor, Pedro's beloved dog, and Amigo, his cousin Rodrigo's.

Many years later, Pedro de Alvarado learned that his dog belonged to a breed called Presa Canario, a race introduced hundreds of years before by the Roman conquerors in the Canary Islands, now a new Spanish colony in the Atlantic.

Day after day, the brothers and the faithful cousin kept with their unorthodox training in the margins of the river, using wooden swords, pikes, halberds, and maces.

On their own, the techniques improved and became more sophisticated. Few times they were instructed or supervised by veteran soldiers, now unemployed, returning home from the recently concluded wars against the Saracens who finally, after more than five hundred years, were defeated by the armies of the new emerging nation of Spain. The country would soon enter a new era of expansion, somehow thwarted by the intolerance of the Dominican friars, who were starting to strangle the populace with the menace of the Inquisition, an institution that could seize property and people at the whim of the main inquisitor without recourse to trial.

The more Alvarado and his brothers trained, the heavier Pedro became; his body turned hard and well toned with powerful arms and legs and an imperious countenance made even more so by his golden mane, his blue eyes, and his tanned skin, all complemented by a fine analytical mind. The town offered nothing that could help advance one's career, even less if you were poor and uneducated as most of the inhabitants were. His mind became obsessed with the New World and the many fantasies that he was constantly fed by the many drifters that came across Badajóz. He longed to mature, to become independent so he could sign for one of the many ships crossing the Atlantic. He was desperate because of his difficult family situation. Pedro also started wondering why his father left the Order of Santiago, but he never got the nerve to ask him the reason for his downfall.

Chapter 3

The celebrations in honor of *Akna*, the mother of fertility, and Chaak, the rain, were in full swing in K'umarkaj, the capital of the K'iche kingdom. The atmosphere was carefree, and the populace was happy.

Many years had elapsed since that fateful day when Tecún-Ahau Galel was born. He was now engaged with his lifelong friends Ixpiyacoc and Vukub discussing the results of the latest games of the just recently concluded ball championship of the kingdom.

The trio was ardent followers and sometimes participants in the games. They were reminiscing the way their favorite team had won the final match. Vukub was the most vociferous, mimicking the last goal of their team that gave the victory.

Prince Ahau's mind kept drifting to his impending encounter with Princess Ixchel, goddess of the moon, to whom he had been betrothed from birth, an alliance made by his and her parents as was the custom within the Maya nobility. Every time they met, his mind went into a tailspin, his speech became difficult, his hands got sweaty, and his heart threatened to jump out of his chest. He was always rendered speechless by her beauty and poise. They had agreed to meet in the central court of the temple of Tojil, the jaguar god. He knew that Ixchel was certainly a sight for sore eyes, a most beautiful lady.

"Hello, Tecún," his friend Ixpiyacoc called him. "Man, you really are in love with Ixchel. I cannot believe your transformation—not that you ever were the light of any party. But still, man, you have *fallen* hard," his friend concluded teasingly. Tecún responded without hesitation, "Look who is talking about falling in love. I know you are sweet on K'etzalin, the sister of my lovely Ixchel. Don't even attempt to deny it because I have seen the way you look at her when she is around. What do you think, Vukub?" He further questioned his other friend, "Am I right, or what?" Despite his bronzed skin, Ixpiyacoc's face became red like an overripe tomato, and he quickly changed the subject.

The central court of the temple was an enormous garden planted with hundreds of exotic flowers of different colors and varieties; among which, beautiful white orchids were prominently displayed. Hundreds of long-tailed ferns lent an air of serenity to the place. The gardens were open to the public with the idea of providing the faithful a place for meditation and peace. The three friends were walking toward the site of the meeting where Ixchel, sitting with her mother, Ixmucané, immediately sensed his presence, sending her heart into a soft and exquisite flutter, her emotions going into a wild frenzy. Even when she was expected to marry the groom chosen by her parents, she knew that she was trapped in the webs of love.

She already knew she loved Tecún more and more every day.

Ixchel considered herself a lucky maiden because she had a man she was madly in love with, who was handsome, tender, considerate, brave, but polite and smart. She was positive Tecún loved her as much as she loved him, which made her happiness more complete. She silently thanked Ah Muzencab, the god of bees, a deity intimately related to happiness and prosperity. They were lucky! What else could she ask for?

As was the Maya custom, when Tecún approached them, he first greeted Ixmucané, Ixchel's mother, who in turn embraced him with much affection as if he were her own son. He then directed his words to Ixchel and to her sister K'etzalin though he knew all along that those words were mostly for his loved one, Ixchel.

"Princess K'etzalin, Princess Ixchel, what a pleasure to see you both. I'm happy that you are as usual beautiful and radiant," Tekún said, keeping a prudent distance. The Maya were socially shy and reserved, strict in their customs.

After the pleasantries were over, K'etzalin and her mother, Ixmucané, accompanied by Ixpiyacoc and Vukub, started to walk a few paces in front of the couple, who couldn't be more gratified than to have a few precious moments for them. Both had a hard time trying to stay apart, separated; they were so attracted to one another. Both were dying to touch hands, caress each other's face, to explore those forbidden places, to seek pleasure in each other's arms. It was pure torture to be a few centimeters apart, but at least they were together.

Many people passing by greeted them warmly, with affection, and commented at how good and happy they looked. The talk of the kingdom

11

was the impending nuptials. All the inhabitants were eagerly waiting the day of the wedding.

The party soon left the premises of the temple and directed their footsteps toward the palace of Ixchel, where the couple and their friends would enjoy a snack. Once they reached the palace doors, their precious privacy evaporated, being replaced by K'etzalin's bubbly banter. She was also nervous because she had been close to Ixpiyacoc, her paramour; she could not wait for him to tell her that he shared her feelings. But he was such a woozy when women were around.

The evening was a pleasant one, full of teasing, touching on many subjects—the boys talking nonstop about the games, the women dissecting the plans for the wedding. They all enjoyed a close camaraderie. Inexorably, the time to say good-bye for the engaged couple came too soon. Luckily, they were alone.

Ahau, taking her hands, said, "Ixchel, I would like to be with you morning, noon, and night. My days are so empty without you, I'm so happy with you. I feel so at peace in your company. I pray the gods to make the time fly so we can be wed."

Ixchel, full of love, responded, "Ahau, I also wish to see you all the time. When we are together, I feel so complete, so cheerful. My mother teases me that since we've been together, she has to request an audience just to see me. But you know, she loves you so dearly that sometimes I feel *really jealous* of you." Ixchel said this with a flirtatious grin that sent his heart into uncontrolled flip-flops. He was happy, content, fulfilled. Ahau-Tecún was thankful to the gods for giving him this lovely woman, this treasured gift that he knew was priceless.

The lovers kept small banter until he finally left the palace in the company of his friends with whom he continued the conversation, now centered in their next endeavor in the next few days—hunting for deer in the forests close to the city. They were young, vibrant and care-free since the kingdom had been at peace for several years now.

When the group reached Tecún's palace, they parted company, promising to continue the conversation next day.

Chapter 4

With great stealth, the men began moving through the dense pine forest, their soft-soled sandals masking the noise of their approach. The party of hunters was headed by Ahau Galel, Prince Tecún, heir to the throne of the K'iche Empire. For many days, the group had been following a herd of deer led by an imposing stag with unblemished skin, high ants, and fleet movements.

Tecún, moving downwind with extreme precision, noiseless, had closed the gap separating him from the animal to less than one hundred feet. His prey was a superb creature, majestic and fully grown. Tecún felt a stab of remorse at having to kill such precious specimen, but his instinct of hunter prevailed.

The animal sensed his presence; it kept prickling its ears, sniffing the air, but could not localize the menace. Maybe it knew its life was about to end.

With utmost care, Tecún selected a sharp obsidian-headed arrow, fit it in the bow's nook, stretched the string of hemp to the maximum range, then, holding his breath for a few seconds to slow his heart, let the arrow fly; the missile flew true and with a sickening thud, penetrated the chest of the buck, piercing its heart. The animal showed surprise and bewilderment at his attacker and soon collapsed to the ground.

With great reverence, in silence, the prince and his companions thanked Jacawitz, the mountain god, for allowing him the honor and privilege of a great hunt. After a few minutes of quiet, a great cheer erupted from the men in his party when they saw the big animal lying dead. Shortly, after a brief hesitation, Tecún unsheathed his obsidian knife and with great skill removed the pelt from the creature, adding it to several more carried by the porters. On their return to town, the skins would be cured and later used for making coats for the cold season, which sometimes brought frost to the highlands. The hide would also be used for fitting shields used during military exercises or actual battles, although the three friends had not been tested in actual combat.

Ixpiyacoc, his longtime friend, always the teaser, exclaimed, "Tecún, you got yourself a big trophy. Now you can run down the mountain and show it to Ixchel and tell her how great a hunter you are." The prince responded, "My dear friend, enough is enough. I know you are envious of my prowess. You are really upset because I bested you! Otherwise, by now you would be scampering downhill to tell K'etzalin about your great skills. Yes, I know you are in love with her but are too afraid to tell her your feelings. Am I wrong?"

After a few more minutes of teasing, Tecún said, "Let's prepare some meat for dinner." Then in a jocular mood he said, "I think I deserve a drink of *chicha.*" *Chicha* is a fermented brew prepared with tamarind, maize, yeast, and sugarcane that rendered a pleasant, slightly tangy beverage, a quite common form of hooch used by the populace as well as by the nobility.

The thick pine forest where they were camped extended for miles in all directions, with some areas so dense that the only way to move through it was by using the tracks carved by the wild beasts over hundreds of years.

The air was balmy, pleasant, scented with the fragrance of grass, wild berries, and pine cones. The view was spectacular. In the distance far away, the river Olintepeque could be seen flowing peacefully away from K'umarkaj.

The hunters continued their conversation late into the night until finally they succumbed to a well-deserved sleep; in few minutes, the only sounds heard were their snoring mixed with the growls of the big cats—the jaguars and the pumas.

The incessant cacophony of the birds announced a resplendent morning; the sun was shining bright, a soft breeze moving the grass like waves in a lake.

High in the sky, a solitary quetzal kept station, guarding his precious charge, Prince Ahau Galel-Tecún.

Even when the Maya were a pacifist nation, the *ajaw* men were splendidly trained. They could endure long marches or run for miles without respite. The specter of war was always a constant menace from the neighboring kingdoms of the K'akchiquels and the Tz'utujils, for many years their enemies. Tecún could still remember when his father was killed during one of these reoccurring wars.

During the splendor of the Maya culture, these three groups were as one, but sometime in the not too distant past, the K'akchiquels, feeling slighted (nobody knew why), left the alliance. They moved west, where they founded their capital, Iximche, a new dwelling in the mountains, which in a short fifty years became a bustling metropolis rivaling the splendor of K'umarkaj. For their part, the Tz'utujils, following the example of the dissidents, moved east to build their own capital, Chuitinamit by the shores of the great lake called Atitlán, present-day Santiago Atitlán. The three kingdoms shared a common language, a common bloodline, a similar style of government, and an equal array of casts.

The K'akchiquels were a bellicose group, forever finding an excuse to start a new war despite that most of the times they were defeated by the K'iche. The Tz'utujils always followed their lead.

Tecún's reverie was cut short when his chief gamer informed him that the camp was closed and they were ready to move whenever the prince decided to do so.

The party departed, bound for the capital, K'umarkaj. The porters were carrying all the pelts they had accumulated during their foray. The hunters only killed the animals considered good game, a challenge to their skills. They did not kill for the pleasure of killing. The animals of the forests were considered sacred and were only sacrificed during the hunt season; besides, the Maya were mostly vegetarian, eating corn, black beans, soy, plantain, and cacao. Ahau Galel, Prince Tecún, was anxiously counting the miles until he reached the metropolis. He was anxious to see Ixchel; he could hardly wait to be with her. She had become his guiding light, his most brilliant star. Despite that he had never caressed that beautiful face; her luminous eyes kept intruding in his thoughts. Tecún could, with his eyes closed, picture that sculptural body. He could feel in his hands that silky hair that moved like the grass when she walked. The intricately woven *huipil* (An exquisitely hand embroidery, sleeveless tunic) could not disguise the curves of her body. Ah, man! He was in love, desperately enamored of her; he did not mind. What else could he ask from the gods?

Tecún could hear the voices of his friends walking by his side, as if they were talking from a great distance; whatever they were saying was lost to him.

After two days of grueling march, the party reached the city, and Tecún was soon at his palace. The steward, being alerted by an advance group, was waiting for him with a cup of fresh lemonade and ordered the other servants to bring some fruits for his lord. In the same breath the steward reminded Tecún that in the early evening he was expected at the palace of Ixchel for an informal dinner, as if he needed any reminder to see the love of his life; fat chance of him forgetting about that!

His personal valet had already chosen the clothes he would wear for his visit with Ixchel. Tecún was to don a short kilt, with a small knife, the shaft made of the finest obsidian and the handle carved from a hard wood called *chichipate*, a tree that grew in the *cerros*, mountains of the kingdom. His chest would be bare; he did not like jewelry. His feet would be encased in soft brownish sandals. For the chill of the evening, he would sport a dark vest spun from the finest cotton. Once his valet stopped fussing about him and left his quarters, Tecún took a long bath, relaxing his muscles and his sore feet. His mind was still conjuring images of his betrothed Princess Ixchel. When he was ready, Tecún left his palace and started walking toward Ixmucané's palace.

Chapter 5

I xchel, goddess of the moon, was sitting in one of the gardens of her parents' palace, watching the birds splashing in the fountains; she was enjoying their colorful, shiny feathers, listening with delight at the cacophony of their chirping. Her mind kept drifting on and off, thinking about her betrothed, Prince Ahau Galel-Tecún.

They had been engaged for a long time, practically since birth, waiting only for her to come of age; she was only a few months short, almost fifteen Venus cycles.

Her sister, K'etzalin, favorite of Quetzalcoatl, approached silently, gliding graciously toward Ixchel, who did not notice her presence until her sister was almost touching her. K'etzalin, in a sweet voice, full of teasing, asked Ixchel solicitously, "My dear sister, where are you? Your mind was miles away, lost in the heavens, close to Tepeu, our creator. Is something worrying you?" K'etzalin kept going, "Don't tell me, were you perhaps thinking about that handsome devil of yours?" She further stated with feigned innocence, "Are you maybe wondering if he is back from his hunt? Or is he delayed or maybe he forgot your invitation. She continued smugly, "Don't worry; he is back in town after he killed the biggest deer in the mountain. News of his great feat has already made the rounds of the gossip circle." K'etzalin had learned of the tidings from one of the kitchen helpers.

Ixchel pouted; everybody but her knew. She said at the same time, "It's not that. I'm afraid for his safety. One of these days he may encounter a party of our enemies, the K'akchiquels or the Tz'utujils, who will attack or kill him." She continued, "I don't understand why they hate us so much. Do they resent our prosperity? No one I ask can give me an answer as to why they came apart from us. I have asked our mother, I have questioned Kakupatak, even I grilled Yum Kaax, who is supposed to know everything about the affairs of the kingdom, but no one can give me a response. It is infuriating."

"My sister, do not fuss, no harm will come to him. You know he is quite capable of defending himself. Besides, his loyal friends Ixpiyacoc and Vukub are always with him, like shadows. Sometimes I think they are brothers. You know very well how loyal to him they are, so much so that they would gladly give their lives to protect him. So calm down, he will be here in no time."

The two sisters continued their exchange for some more time.

The daylight was fading. The time to go in came fast. On entering the *perystilum* of the palace, their mother, Ixmucané, greeted them with a smile. "Ah, there you are. I thought I had lost my two precious jewels," she said with affection. "Come, sit down," their mother said, indicating the soft mats spread on the floor. "I have asked the chef to prepare for us some hot chocolate. He told me that he has some marvelous cacao beans. While we sip our drinks, you can confess all your mischief, all your sins," Ixmucané concluded jokingly.

They were sitting in one of the informal rooms of the palace tastefully decorated with soft colorful mats filled with goose feathers, beautifully embroidered with designs of bees and birds, and weaved from the finest spun cotton; bees were used in many of the clothing weaved by the Maya.

The walls were painted with frescoes depicting breathtaking landscapes. Some of the paintings involved symbols of the house of Hun Hunapú, one of the oldest and noblest families in the kingdom, from which their family descended.

Their exchange continued for some time, touching many topics but always reverting to the theme foremost in their minds, the impending royal wedding. Ixmucané was so happy that Ixchel would soon marry Tecún. He was such a good man! Everybody loved him. She had been waiting for this wedding because she knew that as Ixchel and Ahau grew, they were, as the time passed, attracted to each other like magnets, like moths to the light. Her heart told her that her daughter would be happy beyond measure.

They briefly touched on the alarming news coming from Tenochtitlán, the capital of the Aztec empire, up north, brought in by the *kaweks*. They could still not believe that the emperor Montezuma and his loyal son-in-law, Cuauhtémoc, were engaged in battles against the Tlaxcalans and the Choluteca, their former allies. They didn't know the reason for this aggression. They decided to wait for Tecún so he could shed some light on the matter.

When Ahau-Tecún, arrived, the three women went into a controlled panic, happy, eager, and fusing about him like bees attracted to honey. When Tecún saw their attentiveness, inside he felt a little uncomfortable—he was a humble man. He thought he did not deserve that much attention, but whether he liked it or not, he would shortly become the new man of the house, the new patriarch. He wondered briefly, *I'm so young. How can I fill the big shoes of Ixchel's* Tata?

Gradually, feeling more comfortable, he soon became involved in the discussion, with Ixmucané really grilling him about the news from the empire up north. She made her questions with trepidation, afraid for her kingdom. *Will the same happen here?* She wondered.

"*Nana* (Mother) I am also concerned with this distressing news. What I have heard is that these Aztecs are thirsty for gold, that they have relinquished the promise of equal treatment they made to the Tlaxcalans and the Choluteca when they signed a peace accord. They had become ruthless, abuse their women, using them like slaves; more alarming are the rumors that the conquerors are imposing on these people their rules and their customs. There is talk that these vanquished people are ready for a revolt. We need to get more details. I will question the merchants more in depth." With great tact, he again turned the dialogue to more mundane affairs. Tecún answered their questions about his hunt and told them about the beautiful animal he had felled. He talked about some other relevant events. The evening was passing too fast; he wanted to be left alone with Ixchel, but K'etzalin, as if on purpose, kept talking and talking until finally, mercifully, they were left alone and were able to discuss their own wants.

They were sitting so close that they could feel the warmth radiating from each other's skin. The sweet scent of Ixchel was driving Tecún to distraction, alluring, powerful, but subtle. Tecún longed to touch her, to feel her supple body between his arms, to kiss her soft lips, forever caress that long silky hair. But she was not yet his wife. He would shame her if he broke the rules of propriety. What a nuisance the social norms were, he thought with longing.

The most the couple could do was to casually touch each other's hands, linger a little longer, prolonging the contact, and look into each other's eyes, communicating their feelings silently. Reluctantly, he finally said good-bye. Last-minute endearments were exchanged; each one promised to find a way to see each other soon. Excuses would have to be invented though they really didn't need any pretext; after all, they were already engaged, weren't they?

Chapter 6

"Esperanza, Esperanza. At last we can go to Esperanza," Gonzalo de Alvarado exclaimed. He added, "Pedrito, you are coming with us." The Alvarado brothers had been planning this escapade for quite some time. With great effort, they had saved a few coins, enough maybe to buy some cheap wine and, luckily, the favors of a lady of gracious, easy ways.

The town of La Esperanza would be celebrating the festivities in honor of the Virgin of Sorrows, the patroness of the city. "What a good time we will have," Gonzalo said. He was the oldest of Pedro's brothers.

Esperanza was the town next to Badajóz, a few miles away; it was a larger enclave, more sophisticated, with better-dressed people, more refined and elegant. Some noble families, along with the archbishop, made their home there. The houses were larger and better maintained, the streets wider. The main plaza had an imposing cathedral, the municipal palace building, and a large police force called *La Guardia* (the guard).

The Alvarado brothers got the tacit approval of their mom and, reluctantly, of Don Diego, their father. After donning their best garments they possessed, the brothers left town early next morning bound for fun, full of plans. The dawn found the party riding toward their destination. They crossed the bridge on the river—their playground—and took the main road. The mood was ebullient, full of the promise of youth.

Despite being poor, their mounts were fine Andalusian horses, slim, with graceful, powerful limbs. Mile after mile, the brothers kept their banter; constantly joking, teasing one to each other. It had being a long time since they were in La Esperanza. Rodrigo Sosa, their cousin, was also riding with them. The party was getting near a hill when Gómez, one of the brothers, reined his horse. Pointing forward, he shouted, "Listen, can you hear that noise?" The rest of the group stopped their horses and listened more carefully. The disturbance sounded like the banging of pots and pans with a stick, mixed with the sounds of a strange language, the baying of the donkeys and other animals, interspersed with some singing and plenty of expletives. The jingle was extremely loud, enough to wake the dead. The cackling of chickens lent a surreal atmosphere to the whole thing. After negotiating a curve, they encountered a sight their eyes could not believe.

The noise was coming from a caravan of carts covered with colorful tarps, with plenty of pots and pans hanging from the sides of the wagons. The few able men of the entourage were pushing the first cart, trying with little success to make the wagon go over the top of the hill. The Alvarado brothers were taken aback, surprised; those people were gypsies! For crying out loud, gypsies—considered by Christians to be untouchables, outcast, thieves, kidnapers, unreliable, cheaters, scum of the earth, unworthy to associate with. A real disgrace for humankind

On seeing the Alvarado, the man in charge shouted, "Hey, amigos, could you help us to push these carts over the hill?"

Not a single one of Pedro's party moved; they were frozen.

How could a gypsy ask for their help, let alone address them? They were Christians; they were not supposed to even look at them. Unbelievable! The nerve of those people!

Pedro de Alvarado, despite his youth, took charge of the situation and ordered his siblings and cousin to lend a hand.

"Come on, Gonzalo, Rodrigo, push the wagon. These people need our help." With great reluctance, all dismounted their horses, applied themselves to the task at hand, forgetting for the time being their differences. One by one the carts were brought over the incline. The women of the caravan were surreptitiously watching the strangers do their work. Once the deed was done, the man in charge of the cavalcade came toward Pedro, extended his hand, which Pedro took without hesitation, and said, "My name is Sancho, and this is my family. We are en route to Santiago de Compostela for the celebrations in honor of the patron of the town, the apostle Santiago." He continued, "As soon as we find a suitable spot to camp, you and your family are invited to dine with us." They all remounted their horses and joined the entourage, which started to move, resuming the noise.

After a few miles of march, the caravan found an open flat space with plenty of grass for the animals, with a small creek nearby and some large trees to provide some shade. The brothers saw their chance to get a free hot meal, and gypsies or no gypsies, they had accepted the invitation.

The women were attired with dresses of bright, gaudy colors, some of them, especially the young, with blouses that showed plenty of generous cleavage. Most of the girls had green or blue eyes, light auburn or blondish lengthy hair, long slim limbs, and graceful movements. When Pedro saw that some of the young girls were going to the river to get some freshwater, he offered his help and went with them. One of the women addressed Pedro in a pleasant, lilting Castilian—another surprise, she could speak his language. She said, "I'm Sarita, thank you for your help. Sancho is my father and the elder of my tribe. After dinner, to repay your kindness, I will read your palm and tell your future." Alvarado thanked her and applied himself to the task of carrying water back and forth until enough pails were filled.

The Alvarado watered and fed their horses; they set their own camp a little away from the gypsies. They were still afraid of being robbed. Shortly after, the air was filled with strange aromas coming from the cooking pots. In few minutes, they were invited to join the group for dinner. The young girls served food first to the elders and then to the rest of the men until finally they served themselves and sat in the soft grass, mingling with the guests, talking freely without inhibitions, relating stories about their travels, the places they had been to.

They were so open, without malice, friendly, and extremely beautiful. As Pedro had discovered before, in addition to their dialect, they could speak Castilian, some Basque and Portuguese whereas the Alvarado only spoke their rough Castilian, with the thick accent of Badajóz. The young maids kept sending furtive glances at their guests, teasing them with their eyes. The Alvarado were ecstatic with the food; never in their lives had they tasted such delicious dishes with pungent aromas and fragrant spices unknown to them. During dinner, a bottle of wild berries wine was passed around, and later on, some of the folks played the guitar, singing beautiful, haunting songs that spoke of crossed lovers, lost romances, and faraway lands.

Pedro noticed that some of the men and some of the old women were smoking leaves that produced a heady scent. He went to Sancho and inquired, "What are you smoking?"

"We are smoking tobacco, a plant that comes from the New World, the same with some of the spices used for cooking. Tobacco costs a fortune, if you have to pay for it," Sancho said casually, winking his right eye at Pedro. Sancho offered some to his young guest, but Pedro declined the offer.

Once dinner was over, the dishes washed, Sarita came looking for Pedro; they sat in the steps of her wagon. Then without the least inhibition, she took his hand, tracing the lines of his palm, and intoned in a sweet, grave voice, mature for her age, "I see in your future many adventures. You will travel to a land few have seen before. Your love line predicts that you will have two loves, but only one of them will give you happiness and a new family, different. In time you will become rich and famous, powerful, but your actions will cause a lot of pain and suffering. I'm afraid for you because your temper will bring many unpleasant moments in your life. Be careful with your heart. Try to be generous. I see that the apostle Santiago will always protect you, and you will build and name a new city in his name." She wanted to say more but saw the alarm and dismay in Pedro's eyes and decided to stop there despite the urgings of Pedro, who asked her to keep telling him more. Sarita responded that she could see no more. But Pedro knew she was not totally truthful.

Alvarado was mystified, subdued. How could this young girl tell him such outrageous tidings? After all, she was only a gypsy, and they were only going to the nearest town of La Esperanza to have a good time. But he decided to keep silent and after few minutes of reflection showed his appreciation to Sarita, wishing her a pleasant evening. He went in search of his brothers.

That night Pedro could not sleep; he kept tossing and turning thinking about the words of Sarita. It was true, his father had been a member of the Order of Santiago, but Pedro himself did not believe in saints. After a few hours, he was able to fall asleep, but his sleep was fretful. He kept tossing through the night.

The next morning, the crowing of the roosters and the voices of the gypsies woke the brothers; the travelers were dismantling the camp, getting ready to go on their way.

After a free, succulent breakfast, the siblings helped to take down the camp and said good-bye to their newfound friends; they declined the offer of Sancho to travel with them to Compostela, still marveling at the hospitality of the gypsies. They hadn't expected much from them. The tribe knew more than the siblings, were more illustrated, spoke several languages; their women were cultured, and some of them could read and write, something unheard of in their native Badajóz. Pedro found that they were not as bad as the reputation they had; they were normal, happy, and open, with few inhibitions, with a new way at looking at the union between woman and man. In short, he concluded, they were nice, hardworking, though unorthodox in their thinking. They were not even robbed; they still could count the few coins in their purses.

Jorge, one of Pedro's brothers, could not keep quiet about his experience with one of the gypsy girls, someone named Isabel, who had taken him to her wagon to spend the night with her. Jorge was telling his siblings that Chabelita had been an expert in intimate relations and had taught him many new ways to make love in the short hours they were together. Jorge was so smitten with Isabel that he was willing to one day come back and ask her to marry him.

The encounter with these people had changed the provincial way they looked at the world. Now they knew that many places and people existed beyond the boundaries of their native land. Now they were seeing the downtrodden gypsies with some new respect.

Pedro was also reminiscing on his own experience, how Sarita had read him enchanting poems that told of distant, sometimes fictitious places that spoke of unrequited love. He found himself surprised that he was composing verses in his mind that bespoke of the beauty of his companion of last night. He made a mental vow that one day he would learn to read and write better so he could write down the thoughts that crossed his mind. He had to find a way to accomplish this task on his return to Badajóz. But how could he manage to do this? They were as poor as church mice. Nevertheless, Pedro promised himself this would become his quest. His father knew how to read and write but was always unavailable. The priest, another candidate, was out of the question since they parted company in not the best of terms. Pedro still resented the flogging he got from that infernal crow, that stinking, filthy cleric.

Mile after mile, they kept the conversation, teasing, enticing, joking among themselves, promising to have a fine time in La Esperanza. They were hoping that with their meager savings they would be able to fulfill their fantasy, to maybe meet some local girls and find love in their arms. All was possible in their young, eager minds even when they were small farmers and poor to boot.

Chapter 7

Ihen Pedro's party reached La Esperanza, the celebrations were in full swing. The streets were choked with people, all running toward the central plaza. Since they didn't know the town's layout, the siblings decided to follow the throngs. There were hundreds and hundreds of celebrants, locals and out of town, most dressed in their finest clothes, some not so, like the Alvarados? who suddenly felt underdressed.

Women covered their heads with splendid *mantillas* (a shawl like) with intricate brocaded patterns that framed resplendent blue or green eyes with long eyelashes. Many ladies were using *abanicos* (fans) wielded with expert dexterity with short, snappy flicks of the wrist that showed the face behind, and then rapidly hid it. Men wore *boinas*, dark floppy hat with colorful woven balls sewn at the crown in a form that allowed it to move freely to the right or to the left of the cap as the owner walked.

The noise of the crowd was overwhelming, loud, with many accents from the different regions around the town. All the revelers were excited; rushing to get the best place in the plaza from which they could watch unencumbered the procession of the Virgin at the conclusion of the blessing and the homily given by the archbishop.

The mayor, with other dignitaries of the town as well as many more nobles with their families, was installed in a raised platform. When the Alvarado arrived, the bishop was well into his homily, full of menace, brimstone, condemnation, eternal damnation, but not a single word of hope for redemption or admission to the pearly gates of heaven—too bad, most of the people could not understand the peroration because it was spoken in Latin, at that time the universal language of the Catholic Church. Nevertheless, all attendees pretended to be following every single word. They were afraid of the watchful officers of the holy office for the preservation of the faith—the inquisition—which kept the faithful in a grip of holy terror.

Pedro and his brothers, by pure chance, almost a miracle, landed in a corner of the dais from which they were able to watch almost unobstructed all the proceedings and the important people seated up high.

Unconsciously, Pedro's eyes found a beautiful face with large golden eyes like a tiger's, with long eyelashes, small dimples in her rosy cheeks, a pouting mouth with lips like carnations. Pedro was jolted when those alluring eyes locked on his, sending powerful undercurrents of desire, of a need to get closer to this enchanting creature. At the same time, Pedro was shocked at the audacity of the girl to look at him directly, unflinching, as if daring him to come closer. Pedro promised himself that he would devise a way to find out who she was. Regrettably, to Alvarado's consternation, the sermon continued on and on for a long time, the words pouring from the mouth of the priest like water from a fountain; then, mercifully, to the relief of the listeners, the cleric ran out of breath and concluded his speech.

In a whisper, Pedro told Rodrigo, his cousin, standing by his side, "Did you see that fair lady, the one with the green dress and eyes like an angel?" pointing discreetly at the girl of his interest. He further added, "I have to find a way to meet her. When she comes down from the platform, let's follow her."

Once the enchanting woman came down from the dais, Pedro and his cousin started the chase. Pedro hurriedly told his brothers that he would meet them later on at the inn where they were staying.

Surreptitiously, the two cousins followed her entourage, which shortly made a stop in one of the gardens of the plaza, as if on purpose, Pedro thought. Without losing a second, Alvarado went in search of his mysterious lady; when he came closer, he removed his hat, showcasing his impressive golden mane, bowed slightly at the waist, and in a deep voice, sure of himself, said, "Fair lady, my name is Pedro de Alvarado y Contreras, at your feet." He then graciously took her hand and softly kissed it, inhaling the sweet perfume emanating from her skin. The damsel promptly recovered from her surprise, responding, "I'm Raquel Fuentes, nice to make your acquaintance." Pedro, in a flash, introduced his cousin Rodrigo Sosa. After a few more minutes of conversation, Raquel informed Pedro that she was to have lunch with the archbishop, which she clued him was her uncle, but afterward she would be coming back to church and

0

would like to see him again. The new friends agreed to get together in the early afternoon in the premises of the cathedral.

Alvarado was beyond himself, really happy. He could not thank enough his good fortune to meet this lovely lady. He briefly wondered how Sarita, that gypsy girl, had known that he would encounter this awe-inspiring woman. Amazing! Unreal!

The afternoon kept dragging; the minutes passing with the sluggish motion of molasses, one by one, making Pedro fret with anxiety while he waited to meet Raquel. Together with Rodrigo, they retraced their steps looking for the hostel where they agreed to meet with his brothers. The cousins were replaying the fortuitous encounter, making plans for the new rendezvous. *Maybe,* Rodrigo thought, *she has a friend or a cousin that I can also meet.*

When the pair turned the corner, they found themselves watching a brawl, which initially they tried to bypass, when suddenly a raspy voice called them. "Pedro, Rodrigo, help us," his brother Gonzalo implored. "These ruffians want to kill us. I don't know why, we have done nothing to provoke them. They attacked us without any provocation on our part. I think they are drunk and are only looking for a fight." Soon, Pedro and Rodrigo joined the melee, dispensing blows left and right, making the best use of their informal training back home.

Without any warning, one of the attackers pulled his sword form the scabbard and went after Jorge, attempting to pierce his heart. On seeing this, Jorge, with great speed and skill, produced a long dagger that deflected the sword of his assailant and went to bury it in the chest of the victim. The wounded man fell to the ground clutching his punctured chest, blood flowing from the wound. Observing this, his friends started shouting, calling the guard, "Killers, killers! They have killed my brother! "*Help, help*" The clamor was soon picked up by the onlookers. The mob was becoming uglier and uglier, full of menace and swearing gross words. The shouts for the guard became louder, picked by more and more people who sensed a disaster, claiming revenge for something many didn't know, but all the same, they were clamoring revenge against the estrangers. The mob already had detected their rough accent.

With great aplomb and determination, Pedro grabbed his brother Jorge, who was paralyzed, stuck to the spot, ordering the rest of his party to scamper and try to get away. The *Guardia* had responded promptly and, together with the rabble, started to follow the fugitives; the chase was on.

The Alvarado ran, trying to escape, making many twists and turns, getting lost in the unfamiliar streets until finally they reached the inn. They had temporarily lost their pursuers. Hastily the escaped men saddled their horses and took to the road, making a speedy getaway.

Unfamiliar with the layout of the city, by mistake they found themselves riding toward the port of Cádiz instead of going back to Badajóz. When they realized their mistake, it was too late, and the Guardia were hot in pursuit. They could retrace their steps, but the ugly bunch of people had God knew what plans for them. The brothers were frantic, afraid, trying to put as much distance as was possible. Luckily, their horses were faster than the ones being ridden by the soldiers and the remains of the crowd that little by little lost interest in the hunt. Finally, the fugitives were lost in a cloud of dust. They were safe for the time being.

Chapter 8

PORT OF CADIZ, SPAIN

Running for their lives after the debacle at La Esperanza, where Jorge de Alvarado, by pure accident, apparently killed a man during the fiesta, Pedro de Alvarado and his brothers arrived at the port of Cádiz, in the Mediterranean sea, looking for sanctuary with their uncle Alejandro and his wife, Sara, whom they had never met before. The Alvarado knew that their uncle Alejandro had been living in Cádiz now for several years working as a carpenter. He had repeatedly invited his nephews and his sister, Mexia, to come and live with him and his wife in the port, where they could easily find work. In more than one occasion he had mentioned that he could take them as carpenter apprentices, but they never made the trip until now, forced by the events in La Esperanza.

Cádiz was an ebullient city, full of people from all walks of life, many nationalities—Greeks, Turks, Arabs, Jews, Venetians—hundreds of drifter soldiers from the recently concluded war against the Moors who suddenly found themselves discharged or unemployed, lured to this port by the prospect of enrolling in one of the many expeditions leaving for the New World, called the Indies. All wanted to become rich, maybe even famous. It was late in the afternoon when they reached the port. The streets were filled with throngs coming and going, some of them without any apparent purpose.

The Alvarado brothers got lost many times, but after asking many passersby for directions, they finally reached the home they were looking for. The property was situated on a hill, overlooking the blue waters of the ocean and a magnificent view of the bay, with a well-tended garden, a large stable for the many animals, including horses, a small dog, chickens, and ducks.

The small dog announced their arrival with loud barks until finally his owner, Alejandro, opened the door of his house. He was taken aback when he saw his nephews and Rodrigo. He was speechless trying to explain their presence but happy to see them after many years of being absent from his land of Badajóz. After introducing his wife, Sara, to the rest of the family, Alejandro reiterated his offer of taking them in. They were invited to dinner, during which Gonzalo, the oldest, informed him of their close escape from La Esperanza; he told him and Sara about the accidental stabbing that Jorge inflicted on an unknown person. Alejandro was made aware that the Guardia had followed them. Gonzalo and the rest added their own take on the incident. After hearing the ghastly news, Alejandro reassured them that they would be safe in Cádiz but should keep a low profile for a while. He restated his offer of getting employment for them as carpenter apprentices. He mentioned that there was a great need of carpenters, smiths, cooks, bakers, all kinds of trades to man the many ships waiting to sail overseas. They would go to the port in the morning.

Alejandro inquired about his sister, Mexia, and was saddened because she had not come with them. He missed her.

To complement the excellent dinner prepared by Sara, a good quality wine was enjoyed by the newly reunited family. The siblings complimented Sara on her skills as a cook and marveled at her grace as a delightful hostess. Sara turned to be a young maid for his uncle's age, extremely beautiful, gracious, educated, full of spunk, and extremely friendly. She was taken by the blond mane and deep-set blue eyes of Pedro, his port, and demeanor. She also noticed that he was brooding, grim, sullen. She wondered what happened to him, what the reason was for his despondency.

After dinner, Pedro and Rodrigo offered to help Sara to pick up and wash the dishes. Pedro noticed that the small dog kept quiet at Sara's feet but was extremely alert. Once the chores were finished, Alejandro asked Sara to read some poetry for them, which she did in a sweet and melodious voice, bringing tears to the eyes of the listeners with the poem she was reading. Later on, she took a small guitar and sang beautiful melodies that filled their hearts with longing for the house they unwillingly left behind.

Pedro was really smitten with the many talents of Sara, especially with the fact that she was able to read and write. He was in awe of this young gal. Late at night, the fugitives were shown to the spare rooms of the house and were soon sleeping comfortably.

The next morning, Alejandro left for work. The brothers were given the tour of the house with Sara being a consummate gardener that knew the names of all the flowers and plants of her garden. Later on, she showed them the stable. Pedro and his brothers complimented her on her abilities and again thanked her for her hospitality. She reciprocated by telling them that her husband was really happy to at last see their stranded nephews and their cousin. She reiterated that they were welcome to stay as long as they wanted. The Alvarado were overwhelmed by the selflessness of Sara. Pedro had noticed that Sara commanded her dog with silent signals, and later on he questioned her about this. He told Sara that he had a dog back home, and he missed it a lot. He was so trusting of Sara that he told her about his failed romance with Raquel when they had to run to save their lives. Sara listened with patience and tried to cheer him up.

When Alejandro returned from work, he informed them that a large flotilla was anchored in the bay waiting to depart for the island called Hispaniola and that the chief of the group was indeed looking for people to work in the ships, even, if they were willing, sail with the expedition.

During dinner he told them that he had found employment for them as his apprentices after he had spoken with the man in charge of the fleet, whose name he said was General Hernán Cortés. During the conversation, he also mentioned that the date of departure of the ships was unknown because the enterprise had not as yet found sponsors to fund it. He further said that the lenders of previous sailings had been disappointed with the low profits of preceding voyages. In a soft voice he added that the situation was made worse when the Jews, the biggest lenders, were expelled from Spain when they refused to convert to Catholicism as decreed by the new sovereigns of the new nation of Spain, Fernando and Isabella, the former monarchs of Aragon and Castile, who finally were victorious against the Moors, who had occupied their lands for more than five hundred years. Many Jews had left Spain, bound for Rome when they were offered sanctuary in Rome by the newly elected pope, Rodrigo Borgia, in exchange for exorbitant contributions to his coffers supposedly to benefit the social works of the pontifice but were instead used to buy favors with the other cardinals.

Days turned into months. Alejandro and his nephews left early for work at the docks. With their newfound income, the siblings were able to buy more fashionable clothes, shoes, better swords, and daggers. Pedro bought an enormous sword forged from the finest steel from Toledo, a rival to the damascene swords he had seen before. The soldier who sold the weapon to Alvarado marveled at the ease with which he handled the massive sword. In turn, they became good friends. His name was Juan Argueta, who later decided to stay in Cádiz and maybe sail with them for the New World. Argueta became his eternal companion, forever following him, like a puppy.

Pedro and Sara developed a good friendship, he always respecting the boundaries of decorum for his uncle's wife. Despite her youth, Sara ran the house without a glitch. With time, Sara drew out more details that could explain the sadness of Pedro, encouraging him to be patient. At his petition, she read for him poetry, and soon, Pedro was dictating the poems that he composed in his mind. He asked Sara to help him improve his skills in reading and writing. He also pestered her to teach him the silent signs with which she directed her dog. Pedro was mesmerized with this expertise of hers. Alvarado told Sara about his dog, Valor, left at home; he was afraid that he would never see the mastiff again. Pedro wondered if his mother was taking care of the dog. He also missed her tremendously. He wished she could join them in this newfound heaven of Cádiz.

One evening, when the workers returned from work, Sara came running with great agitation. They asked themselves if something had happened to her. When Sara came closer, she took Pedro's hand and ran to the patio, at the back of the house, telling him with short gasps, "I have a surprise for you and Rodrigo," full of mischief.

When they arrived at the patio, Pedro sighted his mastiff, Valor, who came bounding toward him with powerful strides. Pedro was speechless, unable to believe his eyes. Finally he embraced his friend that by now had become a huge beast.

Soon, both dog and master fused together, like a single unit. Both were jumping with joy, Pedro crying tears of happiness. Shortly, Rodrigo was also hugging his dog, Amigo.

After his excitement abated, Pedro found that the carrier of such good deed was his brother Hernando. On questioning, Hernando informed them that the militia was still looking for them, that they could not return to Badajóz unless they wanted to end up being prisoners of the law.

He said, "Our mother sends her love and blessings. She is sad because she says she would never see you again. She is especially worried for you, Pedro, because you are the youngest, but she refuses to leave our dad, who is about to lose the farm for lack of payment of the rent. Now he is drinking more and more."

During dinner, once Alejandro was apprised of the events, the brothers Alvarado decided to send money to their parents to help alleviate their economic straits. Another decision was reached. They all agreed to enroll in the voyage to the New World. Alejandro promised to speak with General Cortés and secure a place for them aboard one of the ships.

With the skills they had acquired, Alejandro was positive employment would be found for them.

In their spare time, Pedro and Rodrigo continued training their dogs, by now using the silent commands Sara had taught them. They ran in the sand, cavorted in the shallow waters of the beach, daily improving their endurance. Pedro became stronger and more dexterous with the sword and the pike.

One evening, during dinner, Alejandro told the brothers that he and Sara had decided to join them in the venture. They took that decision because the couple didn't have any other family and also wanted to try fortune in the new fabled lands; by now, they were convinced that in the New World they could become rich. Surely, building houses for the new émigrés would be a booming business. The only trick left would be to convince the boss of the expedition to take them in when the ships sailed. Even when Alejandro knew Cortés, he was not, by any means, close to him.

Pedro and his siblings kept shadowing Cortés's soldiers during the maneuvers they conducted on the beach, sometimes tailgating the soldiers. They were fascinated watching the militia and the cavalry execute exercises using live ammunition. He was surprised to find that the dogs used in the drills were not afraid of the noise of the harquebus and the cannons. He also noticed the soldiers using flags to direct the troops. It was thrilling. The harquebuses were powerful but extremely noisy.

For his part, Hernán Cortés had been keeping an eye on the movements of the motley group of Pedro and his relatives, paying special attention to the two huge mastiffs being trained by the youngsters. He was spellbound with the way the blond kid ordered his mastiff with hand signals, without a word. He made a mental note to approach the boy and question him about this talent of his. He had to train his dogs with this new technique that could give him another advantage over his prospective foes.

Suddenly, a sonorous cry emerged from the throng nearby watching the exercises, crying for help. A horse had gotten loose and was running in a frenzy toward a knot of people that were paralyzed by terror when they noticed that the horse was aiming directly for a little girl playing by herself in the sand; nobody was moving or even attempting to do something to save the poor baby from being trampled to death by the crazy horse.

With horror, Pedro discovered that unless the infant was removed, the horse would collide with her. Without any second thought, Pedro jumped on his horse, Corazón, urging the noble beast to hurry up, trying to reach the baby before it was too late.

Pedro was spurring the animal to fly, to shorten the distance between the frenzied horse and the child. With a supreme effort, Corazón reached the spot where the toddler was, completely oblivious to her fate, wondering why her parents were screaming at her; finally, with a supreme effort, Pedro reached for the kid, scooping her with his right hand seconds before the panicked beast could crush her. Pedro continued running until he was sure the danger had passed; then with great calm, he went to the terrified parents and deposited the crying infant in their waiting arms. The parents were beyond themselves, ecstatic at the miracle.

After a few more paces on his horse, Pedro dismounted and collapsed in the sand, trying to get his breath back. It had been a close call. He was happy because he had prevented a tragedy; with his eyes closed, Pedro was trying to make sense of the events, wondering how he was able to accomplish the rescue when instantly he detected a shadow looming in his peripheral vision. Immediately he got to his feet, on guard, working to unsheathe his sword, then a powerful voice commanded him to stand down. "Easy, lad," Cortés addressed the rescuer. "What you did took a lot of courage and quick thinking. I thank you for saving that child. My name is Hernán Cortés I command these armies. I would be honored to know your name. Would you join me for a well-deserved cup of wine?" He extended his hand to Pedro.

After his brief discomfiture, Pedro responded, "Sir, I'm Pedro de Alvarado y Contreras, at your service, General. I would be honored to accept your invitation. I appreciate your kind words." Pedro also extended his hand. Inside, he was beaming. He could not believe his good fortune; he was talking to the leader of the expedition, and the leader had invited him to share a cup of wine! Amazing! What he had done was pure instinct, but he was equally happy that his good deed was about to pay dividends.

Cortés and Alvarado directed their footsteps toward the pier from which a small boat took them to the general's flagship. A cup of wine ended with an invitation to dinner. General Cortés regaled Pedro with anecdotes of his fights against the Moors, how he became commander of the mission, his plans and hopes for the trip to the New World.

Cortés, after some hesitation, asked Pedro to explain how he was able to direct his mastiff with silent, hand signals. Cortés was spellbound with the narrative of this talent of his. Alvarado had become a natural-born raconteur; he was more than delighted to comply with Cortés' request. He narrated in great detail the nits and grits of this art, adding some embellishment of his own. Pedro so wanted to prolong this unexpected opportunity. Cortés was so taken by the enthusiasm of the youth that he decided to invite him to join his soldiers in the maneuvers they conducted on the beach on a daily basis.

Alvarado was overjoyed; he could hardly believe his ears at this invitation. In exchange, he promised Cortés to teach his dogs' handlers his trick with the signals. He told himself that he had found his ticket to the new territories; the trick now would be to convince Cortés to take him and his family aboard the ships. All the riches beyond the immense ocean were waiting for him. He promised Cortés to be at the training grounds early next morning. Without a conscious effort, he had succeeded beyond his wildest expectations. Alvarado could hardly wait to reach home and impart the good news to his family. He was so happy.

After some time, Alvarado bid good night to his new protector and departed for home. To him the night looked promising, enchanting, the air sultrier. Was his destiny to sail to the New World? he wondered. Was he old enough to join such enterprise? Pedro felt that the time it took for him to reach his uncle's house was too long; he was raving to impart the good news. He would have to ask Alejandro's advice. Maybe he could enlighten him as to what to do. Would his uncle really come with them? Pedro could hardly wait to be home.

When he finally arrived, Alejandro and his brothers released a breath of relief in knowing that he was back safe and sound. They were overwhelmed when Pedro told them of the offer of General Cortés. The night was short for the many plans each one was making, sometimes shouting his ideas to be heard by the other participants. They were delirious. Even Sara, the most conservative of the group, was really taken with the prospect. *Maybe,* she thought, *I could become a lady surrounded by servants.* All was possible in those distant lands, or so she was led to believe by the rumors.

Chapter 9

Bright and early the next morning, Alvarado and his group were at the beach waiting for the troops of Cortés. Now they were allowed to train on a regular basis with the real soldiers. The siblings learned new tactics, were instructed in the proper use of the swords and pike, and loaded and shot the cumbersome harquebus; they became harder and stronger.

Pedro's swordsmanship improved dramatically; he discovered that he was a natural leader, and the men followed his instructions despite his youth. His mastiff became bigger and meaner and learned new tricks. It could stay silent but alert for long periods of time and spring into action with a subtle hand signal from Alvarado. He taught his new friends all the tricks in his personal repertoire, adding some newfound maneuvers.

Every single day, Alvarado kept devising new ways to convince Cortés that he was the ideal man for the job at hand. He became indispensable to Cortés, always handy to carry his orders. Day by day his conniving methods found a more sympathetic ear with Cortés until one day Hernán caved in and promised Pedro a place in his army. He was enlisted as a minor captain. Cortés told him, "Pedro, you have convinced me of your worth, your spirit, your courage. I have seen you working with great diligence, becoming a better soldier. You have trained my dogs and yours with great zeal." He kept going, "The soldiers like you and gladly follow your orders. When you saved that girl, the men turned in your favor. It took a lot of nerve to do what you did. Your quick thinking avoided a tragedy. You will serve directly under my command."

This was beyond Alvarado's wildest expectations. He was now an officer directly under the big honcho. He could hardly wait to tell his brothers and uncle. He decided to push his luck a little bit more. Pedro answered, "General, you do me honor in asking me to serve under your direct command." He eagerly added, "I will faithfully serve you, our king, and our queen. General, you will not regret your decision."

Pedro was now on a roll. Taking a deep breath, he decided to make his next petition; it was now or never. "General Cortés, you met my brothers, and you know my uncle Alejandro, who is a splendid carpenter. His wife, Sara, is a charming lady and an excellent cook. Would you allow them to join the expedition?" Alvarado finished with a humble bend of his head, waiting for the explosion of his new commander. Instead, Cortés responded affably, "Pedro, Pedro, you drive a hard bargain. You know that I like your uncle, though I have not met his wife, but I'll take your word for it. They are welcome to join the venture." With mirth, he concluded, "Don't forget to include your brothers and cousin, as well as your mastiffs."

The conversation continued for some more time, but Pedro's mind was already beyond the horizon, seeing lush tropical lands encumbered with mountains of gold and gems. He had been voraciously listening to the many soldiers recently back from those lands. He could already picture himself loaded with such treasures. He vowed that one day he would come back to La Esperanza rich and famous and ask Raquel to marry him. She continued to be a fixation in his mind, a sore need in his heart, even though he barely knew her. She had made an indelible impression in his young dreams.

Later on, during dinner, Alvarado gave the good news to his uncle Alejandro, to Sara, his wife, and to his brothers and cousin Rodrigo. Everybody promised to be ready when the time for sailing came.

In the next few days, Alejandro made provisions to rent his home and carpentry shop to a good friend of his. Alejandro and Sara had also become infected with the bug of the rich lands across the sea; they were excited at the prospect that with hard work and time, they too would become rich. He reasoned that certainly a good carpenter would be needed in the new colonies. He was so positive about this. Sara, for her part, was already planning their new home with larger gardens, many horses, and other assorted animals. She also had heard tales of the virgin territories. She had found that there were myriad of trees and flowers still unknown to her. She was excited at the outlook.

After many more months of delays, setbacks, disappointments, Cortés informed them that the archbishop of Cádiz, with the king and queen included, along with other investors, agreed to finance the enterprise. In return for their investment, in addition to the monetary gains, the archbishop insisted that Cortés should convert the heathens to the Catholic faith and the rule of the crown of Spain. The prelate also reassured the monarchs that with bringing the new converts under the Spanish yoke, they would also pay tribute to the sovereigns. A boon for all, except the people soon to be vanquished.

The flotilla finally left the port of Cádiz bound for the island called Hispaniola, present-day Labadie (Labadie) in the Caribbean Sea. From there, the ships would make a final stop in the island of Juana (Cuba), and from there they would set sail for their final destination, the new territories of New Spain (Mexico).

The fleet, before crossing the vast Atlantic Ocean, made a final stop in the recently acquired colony of the Canary Islands by Spain to resupply provisions and to make the necessary repairs before the last leg of the voyage. After several months at sea and the previously planned stops, the armada arrived at the run-down port of Villa Rica in 1519, a rustic enclave first conquered by yet another Spaniard, Juan de Grijalva.

Once there, Cortés found by new information provided by an indigenous group the Totonec, that after many days' march, existed a large city called Tenochtitlán, ruled by a king named Montezuma, extremely wealthy, but cruel with their former allies, the Choluteca and the Totonecs. The ruler of the Totonec promised Cortés fifty thousand warriors to attack their former lord. Cortés, after making great improvements to the port, renamed it the port of Vera-Cruz (Latin for cruz verdadera o cruz real) and then decided to march toward the capital of the Aztec empire, Tenochtitlán. After slaying the ruler Montezuma, he fought against his son-in-law, Cuauhtémoc, who almost defeated him during the battle later known as the Noche Triste (Sad Night) on the days of June 30 to July 1, 1520, during which Cortés was miraculously salved from a certain death by Pedro de Alvarado, one of his favorite acolytes. This act cemented the uneasy friendship between Cortés and Alvarado. Cortés, in gratitude, ascended Alvarado to the rank of captain and later put him in charge of the areas around Vera Cruz.

During his tenure, Alvarado showed his cruel streak subjecting their former allies, the Totonec and Choluteca, to obscene taxes and punishments uncalled for. Finally, Cortés, with the imminent threat of revolt from the Indians, was forced to remove Alvarado from his post. During this dismissal, Cortés tongue-lashed Alvarado for his transgressions and the unjust treatment of these *subditos(subjects)* under his rule. During the dress down, Alvarado was furious, fuming, but kept his temper in check, waiting for a new opportunity. Wasn't he responsible for saving Cortés' life? He was positive he deserved a better treatment from his superior, didn't he?

Hernán Cortés was shortly named *Adelantado* of the valley of Oaxaca and beyond, with his seat in the new city of Mexico, the capital of the realm of New Spain, formerly the site of Tenochtitlán. His new mandate included vast tracks of land to the south of his central command, well beyond the lands of the Totonecs and the Choluteca, the domains of the Tlaxcalans and other parts still unexplored by any white man.

Alvarado continued biding his time but kept his finger on the button; sometimes pushing hard for a new command, other times releasing the pressure, but always trying to carry favor with Cortés, pushing to become his favorite captain, intriguing to be the officer to go to.

Alvarado was restless, impatient, until one afternoon, during one of his meetings with Cortés, Pedro finally mustered his courage, blurting, "General, I would like your permission to deploy our troops south. I have reliable information though it was a stretch of the truth that this lands were rich in gold, silver, spices, pretty women reasons that caught Cortés' attention and heathens that need to be converted to the Catholic faith for the benefit of our esteemed king and queen." Alvarado continued, "Please, allow me to march to those places and bring them under your rule. Besides, the men are getting restless, bored after many months of inaction."

Cortés did not give him an immediate answer and decided to wait, to see if Pedro would desist from this petition. He inwardly thought what *I'm going to do with this young, impetuous captain?* He was becoming a pest, a boil that needed to be lanced, but how? After all, he owed his life to this man. What a grave decision he had to take. Would he later on regret it?

Months went by, and Alvarado kept insisting on his petitions until finally, Cortés, driven to distraction by the constant nagging of Alvarado, after much soul-searching and against his better judgment, appointed Pedro de Alvarado y Contreras as governor of the province of Oaxaca, a minor enclave south of Mexico, formerly the proud city of Tenochtitlán.

The arrival of Alvarado in Oaxaca was a real disappointment. He was expecting a city as imposing as Tenochtitlán; instead Alvarado found a hamlet like, with few structures worth mentioning. Nevertheless, he promptly recovered and got to work, attempting to make his city a better place. Alvarado ordered to build around a central plaza the municipal palace (his palace), a cathedral (against his wishes since he was not a devout man or believed in God), and some other government edifices, like the building for the *Guardia* and other minor offices.

Months later, while sitting in his new quarters, Alvarado received one of his former aides, Captain Cristobal Olid who came with a message from General Cortés. Olid was shown into Alvarado's sanctum. Olid, taking a short breath, addressed his superior, "Governor Alvarado, I have a gift for you from General Cortés." With the approval of Alvarado, Olid continued, "The general had sent with me an Indian princess, the daughter of Xicotenga, the cacique of the Tlaxcalans. Xicotenga gave his daughter to Cortés as a symbol of friendship, but the general, as proof of his good faith for you, decided to give her to you. The princess was recently baptized in the Catholic faith and was given the name of Luisa de Xicontencalt. She has learned Castilian and speaks, besides her own language, other dialects of the people living south of your governorship." Olid added, "Governor, I think she could be useful as an interpreter with these natives. Can I bring her in?" Olid asked this with trepidation since he knew Alvarado's legendary temper.

Alvarado was intrigued. Was this a trick from Cortés? After a brief respite, he commanded Olid, "Very well, let's find out what was I sent, bring her in." Pedro de Alvarado was expecting an old woman, a hag; he was taken aback, surprised, when the princess was shown in. The princess was regal, a pretty gift for sore eyes. Doña Luisa had large dark eyes, vivacious; lustrous jet-black hair, long, almost to her waist; round firm breasts; a solid abdomen; and ample hips with powerful long legs. Her countenance was that of wealth and power, of class. In short, a real indian princess!

Without waiting for permission to speak, in a sweet, soft, well-modulated voice, the indian princess said, "I'm Doña Luisa Xicontencalt; my father is Xicotenga, king of the Tlaxcalans, which has given me to you as a gesture of his friendship and devotion to the king of Spain and the governor of Oaxaca, Don Pedro de Alvarado y Contreras." She had addressed Alvarado in an almost flawless Castilian. Luisa continued, "My lord, I was ordered by General Cortés to come to you and be your loyal helper." She refused to say servant then she bowed with great dignity and grace, respectful but not subservient.

Alvarado, after recovering from his momentary shock at the aplomb and audacity of this woman using his wit, charm, and best manners, directed his words to Luisa, "Princess, I welcome you to my service." He almost said "my bed." Alvarado kept going, "You will be my interpreter with your own people and the people beyond our borders. I understand you are also fluent in other dialects. You will stay in an office close to mine so whenever I need your services, you will come immediately."

Alvarado's mind was already looking for possibilities beyond the purported role of the princess. He already felt attracted to this mysterious woman. Who was she? Could she be used to advance his ambitions? Would she be an asset, or would she be a hindrance?

Alvarado further instructed Cristobal Olid to make the necessary arrangements. Shortly, the princess was given an office next to Pedro's with a door connecting the two chambers. *Perfect,* Alvarado thought.

For her part, Luisa was also thinking of ways to ease the suffering of her people. She vehemently believed her father had made a tremendous blunder in allying his subjects with the Spaniards. Their "allies" had turned into beasts, abusing the women, looting the treasure of her nation, enslaving the men, working them mercilessly on their new farms, lands taken from them. They were so gross and uncouth. The devils also made a mockery of her gods. It was outrageous. She promised to find a way to accomplish her task or perish in the attempt. Doña Luisa possessed a keen mind, devious, cold, calculating. Inwardly she thought that her new master, Alvarado, would be a hard man to cross but very likely could be manipulated. Time would tell.

Chapter 10

A few months after assuming his post as governor, Pedro de Alvarado was still wondering where all the treasures were. Under threats, torture, he had questioned dozens of indians to no avail. Not a miserable gem was found. Where the hell had they hidden their treasure? Alvarado wondered. His men were also displeased, edgy, when no gold was found, not even a single ounce of silver. Had they been deceived?

After yet more brutal interrogations, Alvarado learned that beyond the jungles to the south, an area that the aborigines called The Yucátan existed other kingdoms. Pedro was assured that these people were rich beyond measure, with mines of gold, silver, a greenish precious stone they called jade, and sumptuous palaces. His information was made complete by further questioning many merchants making the trek between those places and Tenochtitlán up north. Alvarado wondered if these details were a massive deception on the part of the natives. He became more obsessed. With these treasures, he could become a rich man. With wealth, he could be famous.

He had to find a way to get there. He obsessed night and day, questioning again and again any source that could corroborate what he had already found.

In 1520, Alvarado sent an expedition with the idea to establish contact with the people of these kingdoms. After long negotiations, the envoys, Cristobal Olid and Pedro Portocarrero, were able to negotiate a peace treaty with Acajal, the cacique of the K'akchiquels, and Xahil, the cacique of the Tz'utujils. Both dignitaries represented people sworn enemies of the larger kingdom of the K'iche up north. Again, Alvarado was told this last kingdom was extremely wealthy. Acajal and Xahil did not tell their new allies that they were also looking for ways to defeat their archenemies and had decided to ally themselves with the Spaniards to fulfill their objective, revenge. They sent Alvarado small caches of gold, few pieces of green jade, some exotic birds and other small animals, but not a single woman as the envoys had requested as a token of good will. As a matter of fact, during their stay in the city of Iximche, the capital of the K'akchiquels, the emissaries did not see a single young maid. Were they hidden on purpose? They saw a lot of mature women and many children. When questioned, the caciques were evasive in their answers.

These small gifts only whetted the appetite of the new governor of Oaxaca. He wanted more, much more, not these small caches that amounted to a pittance.

Pedro de Alvarado started pestering Cortés with petitions requesting to allow him to further explore these fabled lands. Alvarado kept sending dispatch after dispatch, personal envoy after personal envoy, exhorting Cortés to allow him to march toward these domains to finally find for sure if the information he had obtained was accurate or was merely tall tales. After many entreaties, supplications, petitions, veiled threats, and endearments from Alvarado, Cortés finally gave his approval to Alvarado to proceed with his proposal.

He provided Alvarado with some needed money, powder and additional troops, four small cannons, harquebusiers, few more equipment, and some rudimentary maps of the region obtained from the merchants making the trip along the causeway between the Aztec capital up north and the city of K'umarkaj, the seat of the K'iche kingdom, his intended final destination.

Deep down, the real purpose of Alvarado in proposing this opening with the people down south was to acquire more land, claim it in the name of the new king of Spain, Carlos V. In doing so, Alvarado reasoned, the king would look upon him with more favorable eyes and maybe name him an *Adelantado*—a regent like, in charge of larger or more important holdings. The messenger sent by Cortés was specific in the orders he was given by Hernan that this opening was to try to bring these people as allies of the crown and not to wage war without his approval.

Alvarado was somewhat disappointed. He had expected a more broad-reaching endorsement; instead, he had found himself with what amounted to a diplomatic mission. He had to gather all his self-control before he sent for his two trusted captains, Pedro Portocarrero and Cristobal Olid, to instruct them on this operation. He needed all his wits to fabricate and embellish his commission so his two lieutenants would not suspect that he was about to embark on a mission that would be the opposite of what he had proposed to Cortés.

When Cristobal Olid and Pedro Portocarrero entered the office, Alvarado's temper was completely under control. He instructed Olid and Portocarrero on the purpose of the undertaking. At least part of the predictions of Sarita, that gypsy girl, were about to be fulfilled. The stage for his future plans was being slowly built. He was eagerly anticipating this journey. Cristobal and Pedro would be accompanied by a contingent of friendly indians led by Xicotenga, Luisa's father, in whom Alvarado was starting to depend more and more.

The diplomats left early next morning bound for the capital of the K'iche kingdom, the next victim in Alvarado's feverish designs. He was spoiling for a new fight, another adventure where he could prove his manhood and realize his newfound dreams. Alvarado had instructed his minions to put as much pressure on the king of the K'iche and make him accept his peace offer. He was doubtful the cacique would refuse his openings after which Alvarado would follow with more demands.

Chapter 11

Kakupatak, war chief of the Maya kingdom of the K'iche people, was discussing with his Nima—Captain Ahau Galel, Prince Tecún, one of the actual regents of the realm—informing him of the visitors sent by the governor of Oaxaca, a place they had heard of before, waiting to see him. Kakupatak, said, "We have these two messengers waiting to meet with you." He continued, "They say they come in the name of a man called Pedro de Alvarado, whom the Tlaxcalans and Choluteca call Tonatiuh, the sun. They describe him as a pale, tall man with eyes as blue as the sky, his hair the color of maize. His face is covered by golden hair. They insist he is the reincarnation of Quetzalcoatl, the white-feathered serpent."

Kakupatak took a brief respite, then proceeded, "Would you like to see them today, or should I make them wait?" He waited for instructions.

"I wonder what he wants. Is he seeking to make peace as he did with the K'akchiquels and the Tz'utujils, or is he trying to lull us into a peace agreement and then dispossess us? What do you think, Tata?" Tecún inquired from his mentor. Without waiting for an answer, Tecún instructed Kakupatak, "Have them wait, I will see them in two days' time, maybe by then we will know more about them." After some more delay, Kakupatak informed the head envoy, Cristobal Olid, that his lord would see them in two days' time. The emissaries were provided with accommodations in a sumptuous palace reserved for visiting dignitaries. They were given food and beverages, were treated with courtesy as the protocol demanded, but they were confined to their lodgings under an undisguised guard.

The servants tending the foreigners were gossiping about their light-colored skin, colorless eyes, their bearded face, and long brownish hair. Their main comments were directed to the large animal they came riding on, but they were specially taken aback by the two menacing huge black beast that kept quiet, growling softly, sometimes barring large teeth, their eyes constantly roaming, alert, coiled, ready to spring at any moment's notice. Even when the Maya had small *chuchos* (dogs), they had never seen animals like these. They were amazed at the large animal, so docile, beautiful and patient.

Later on, Xicotenga, the Tlaxcala accompanying the envoys, told his guards that the foreigners called the large beast *caballo* (horse) and the short one they referred as *perro* (dog). Upon further inquiry, they found out the dog was a special breed unknown to them, called mastiff, which the foreigners used against their enemies. Xicotenga kept shooting the breeze with his guardians but was not allowed to wander outside his quarters. Their hostesses were also wary of his presence. The K'iche considered him a turncoat, a traitor.

Two days later, as they were told, the Spaniards were ushered into one of the formal reception room. The place was richly appointed with elaborate tapestries and thick, soft cushioned mats, beautiful landscapes painted on the walls, some clay ornaments beautifully painted in ocher and yellow hues.

Prince Tecún and his war chief, Kakupatak, were waiting for them, dressed in their best formal attire, standing with reserved countenance, wondering what the purpose was of this visit. The foreigners were dressed with a silver helmet, a breastplate of the same color, which they had polished to a gleam, a short knife in the left side, and a sword to their right. Later on, Tecún would learn that the knife was called *daga* (dagger) and the long one was called *espada* (sword). With this display, the soldiers were trying to intimidate the waiting dignitaries, but somehow they had failed in their attempt. Tecún and Kakupatak were inscrutable, dignified, waiting patiently, stoically assessing the men.

As was the custom, the messengers did not bow or show respect to their hosts but kept their hands on the pommel of their swords; nevertheless, despite their better training, they were impressed by the imposing figure of Tecún, full of self-confidence and dignity. He was not like the other savages they had met before.

He was well built, with a powerful chest and wide shoulders; his eyes were dark, intense and alert, like a predator. His jaw showed a determination they had not seen before.

Tecún, keeping a watchful eye on the ambassadors, ordered Xicotenga, Luisa's father, who would act as interpreter, to ask the foreigners to state the purpose of their visit.

The man in charge of the mission spoke first, directing his words at the prince with undisguised resentment for the affront of having to wait two days for their audience; he was ignorant or elected to ignore the established protocol. They should have announced their visit beforehand or requested an audience instead of coming without being invited.

"I'm Cristobal Olid, special envoy of the governor of Oaxaca, Captain Don Pedro de Alvarado y Contreras, direct representative of our king, Carlos V. My companions here are Pedro Portocarrero and Sergeant Juan Argueta," Olid said, indicating each one. "Our leader, Governor Alvarado, sends us in peace. He wants to sign a treaty with your people, as he did with your neighbors the Cachiquels and Zutujils," he said, butchering the pronunciation of the kingdoms. Olid continued, "In exchange for your loyalty and the promise of nonaggression, Governor Alvarado, in his infinite wisdom and mercy, demands a yearly tribute in gold and gems, amount to be determined at his discretion. Your subjects will be instructed in our Catholic faith, you will abandon your pagan ways. Your priests will no longer be allowed to preach and pollute the mind of the people with their barbaric rituals. Furthermore, your temples will be transformed into churches where you will worship our Lord, Jesus Christ." Not done yet, he kept going, "Your men will be used in the fields as help." He almost tripped and said "slaves." "Some of your women will help in manual chores," he closed, concluding his demands. Olid, still resentful, had added his own take on the demands.

As the translation proceeded, Tecún's and Kakupatak's eyes flashed with alarm and contempt. Who was this *kajol* (servant) who dared to impose demands on them? They were not yet their slaves. It was outrageous, they thought. Tecún ordered Xicotenga to stop translating, and keeping a direct eye on the intruders, he spoke, "You will tell your lord that the K'iche people do not accept his proposal because it is designed to dispossess us from our dignity, our way of life, our traditions. He wants to make us slaves. Since you are my guests, your lives will be respected. You are to leave my kingdom tomorrow morning. You are not welcome to return unless your disrespectful attitude and the terms of your offer are changed. Otherwise, if you ever set foot in my lands, your lives will be forfeited." With this admonition, he left the room, followed by his war chief. Tecún was furious. He could not believe the gall and rudeness of these devils. They were so uncouth.

The K'iche, still being civil, followed the protocol of hospitality as commanded by Tecún; their lives were spared.

Full of spite and threats, the Spaniards left the capital the same afternoon, vowing, sotto voce, to one day return and make them pay for their insolence and the refusal to accept the "benign" terms of the treaty they were offered. Cristobal Olid and his minions kept openly discussing the results of the meeting, assuming that nobody was able to understand what they so openly were discussing. They were wrong; some of the Tlaxcalans already knew some Castilian and notified the K'iche authorities of the threats proffered. The informers also mentioned that the aggressors were swearing to use against them not only the mastiffs accompanying them but other brutes they had back in Oaxaca. They told that the number of mastiffs was more than twenty, some of them larger than the ones they saw. They especially singled out the huge mastiff belonging to Alvarado. These disaffected informers were trying to instill fear in the hearts of the K'iche. The Spaniards were recording or at least trying to commit to memory the topography of the place with the purpose that when they came back, Alvarado would have at least some idea of the terrain.

The envoys crossed the Olintepeque River at a place where the waters were shallow and the current was slow and pleasant, but the soldiers didn't know that downstream, the current and the depth of the river were different.

Chapter 12

After few days' ride, Olid and Portocarrero returned to Oaxaca. They were positive they had impressed the savages with the horses and the mastiffs they had brought along. They had seen the open-mouthed way the natives had watched the animals. Olid and Portocarrero had seen a few small dogs in the city but nothing as large as their mastiffs.

They also noticed the wonder with which the natives looked at the large horses, fascinated at the way the white men went atop the beasts, how they, with a small rope in the mouth of the animal, could direct it to perform what the man mounted on the creature desired.

The two soldiers had filed in their minds for further reference the dread the natives showed when the large dogs moved, from which they kept at a distance. Now they knew that these animals could be used effectively against the Indians. And they would do it!

As soon as the soldiers entered the governor's palace, the emissaries were ordered to report at once to Alvarado, who was waiting for them after he had been alerted of their return by the watchmen he had posted at the outskirts of the town. The governor was dying to listen to the report.

Without a preamble, he started questioning the men. He was especially interested to know about the palaces, the treasures, any indications that these people were indeed rich as he was led to believe. He grilled them about his prospective opponent, the K'iche cacique. He did not sit; Alvarado was pacing in his office in a state of great agitation and impatience. In a rude way, he ordered the messengers to speak.

Cristobal Olid was the first to speak. "Captain, Governor Alvarado, their cacique, they call him Ahau Galel, but he also goes by the name Tecún, which the natives use more often, he is an impressive man, powerfully built. He looks dangerous, and he seems to be in control of his emotions. Without hesitation, he flatly refused your generous offer. I think he could be trouble. My advice, sir, is to be careful and keep a sharp eye on him," he stated.

"What about your impressions, Pedro?" Alvarado said, turning to Pedro Portocarrero. "What did you see? Are they rich? How do you measure this man? Was somebody else with him?"

After few seconds of hesitation, mostly to frame his report, Portocarrero answered, "Governor, the little we saw of the palace was richly appointed. Even the quarters we were lodged in were extremely luxurious. I saw some indications of wealth well beyond what I have seen before."

Portocarrero continued, "Tecún had a man by his side to which he paid a lot of attention, he probably was his war chief. Though he did not speak, he communicated with his lord with subtle changes in his body movements. I'm positive he might be a hard bone to chew. They both were not afraid of us and showed a great command of their emotions."

On hearing this news, Alvarado went into a rage, showing the dark side of his personality; he kept rambling, threatening retribution, war against these ungrateful heathens. How could they refuse his generous offer of peace and protection? Who did they think they were? Unbelievable!

The men, by now used to these displays, waited patiently for a few minutes until their commanding officer's temper returned to normal, until his fury abated completely.

Alvarado dismissed them. Reluctantly, against his most fervent wishes, he faced the reality that he had to inform his superior, Cortés, of the unsuccessful enterprise they were entrusted with. How he hated to be a failure! His aides were such incompetent fools. Good for nothing, as his father once told him. He was in a quandary. For one, his men were raving for pillage; they were bored and mutinous, wondering what happened with the riches they were promised. Could he keep them much longer?

After a few minutes of reflection, he ordered his amanuensis to write down an official document he would dictate. In great detail he informed Cortés of the failed offering of peace toward the K'iche nation, but he conveniently omitted to mention his unjust offer, instead leveling false accusations against the K'iche king and his war chief, inferring in a veiled manner that these two savages were planning to attack the peaceful nations of the K'akchiquel and the Tz'utujils, their new allies. He further added that the K'iche chieftain had openly mocked and defied the holy mother church—even when Alvarado did not care about the church or religion.

In a daring request, Alvarado asked Cortés' blessing to form an expedition to punish these ingrate savages and teach them the true faith.

Alvarado ordered his secretary to dispatch this letter that day without any delay. He was raving to move down south. His restless soul needed action; his mind craved revenge. The messenger left that same afternoon.

After few days, Cortés received the petition. When he read it, he sensed a trap and decided to wait for some time, to let it simmer down for as long as was possible. Knowing Alvarado's talent for embellishing the truth and blaming others, he reasoned, he could safely delay his response.

For his part, Alvarado was not willing to wait. He kept his demands; he continued sending messenger after messenger. He was eager to bend the defiant K'iche lord. He had vowed to teach them a lesson they would never forget. With the prospect of a future invasion, Alvarado intensified the training of his troops, paying special attention to the preparation of the mastiffs. His beloved dog, Valor, was given particular attention. He exhorted his soldiers to be ready for future action against the heathen K'iche to the south of Oaxaca.

When he heard that some of the most veteran soldiers were grumbling about the lack of action and no payment of their wages for several months, Alvarado again promised his loyal troops untold riches; he convinced even the most recalcitrant ones that the booty was only a few leagues beyond the jungles of the Yucatán. The riffraff were then reassured by Alvarado that he would lead them to new heights, to never-before-seen glories. By now he was delusional, feverishly propping the stage for the next step in his deadly gamble. What's more the pity, he had somehow convinced his most loyal followers, but most especially Sergeant Juan Argueta, who had latched with him while in Cádiz and then again during the campaign against the Aztecs many months ago. Argueta was his gofer, almost his confidant and friend, sometimes his deaf sounding board since Argueta, knowing his master, kept his answers to himself. He didn't need a tongue-lashing. He vented all his fury against Alvarado during the sparring sessions they held together. Argueta had taught Alvarado the best way to handle the huge sword he himself sold to the captain back in Cádiz.

Chapter 13

A few months later, spurred by the insidious encouragement of the Spaniards, the K'akchiquels and Tz'utujils attacked the K'iche. The clash was brutal and bloody with both armies fighting savagely, with no quarter given on either side. The aggressors were supervised by the Spaniards, who kept to the side, watching, making sure Alvarado's orders were carried verbatim.

In command of the K'iche armies was Tecún's grandfather, Don K'iqab, representing the royal house of Tekún, the actual regents of the Empire. He was a seasoned veteran of past conflicts. His deputy was Kakupatak. Don K'iqab directed his troops with great skill, being able to push the invaders to their former borders by the great lake called Atitlán, a large body of water with two majestic volcanoes framing it like ancient sentinels.

Meter by meter, in a supreme effort, the K'akchiquel army pushed their opponent, with thousands of arrows flying, finding their mark with deadly accuracy. The grunts of the fighters added a cacophony to the battlefield. The fight continued for several days more, each side taking turns in partial victories. The hate was intense, no mercy was given and no mercy was asked.

The final push of the K'iche soldiers finally came, applying themselves with renewed strength encouraged by their leaders. When the victory was almost within reach, Don K'iqab was mortally wounded in the chest by a stray arrow, his blood pumping out like a geyser, probably a direct hit to the heart. His life, despite the efforts of his aides, ebbed in a few minutes; he died without knowing that by his efforts and leadership the battle had been won. On seeing the death of his commander, Kakupatak, his loyal deputy, assumed command of the K'iche troops, urging them to avenge the slaying of their beloved leader. In a intense effort, the K'iche were able to subdue the enemy, who immediately asked for clemency. Unfortunately, the instigators of the conflict, Acajal and Xahil, disappeared into the surrounding forest. Their aides, left behind to face the wrath of the victors, accepted their fate and were promptly executed. The defeated troops and many minor officers were forced to return to their previous borders, still simmering with rancor, vowing revenge.

Acajal and Xahil, as soon as they were safe and away from the debacle, complained to Alvarado about the unprovoked attack from the K'iche. They did not mention that they had been the aggressors. Alvarado accepted this version of the events as truth because it fitted to perfection his plan to invade the K'iche kingdom. He had found his excuse.

Ahau Galel, Prince Tecún, was devastated upon learning about the death of his beloved grandfather. Now he knew that the storm was building and that this newfound peace was only a respite.

Don K'iqab's funeral was an occasion of great solemnity as deemed by his rank and his noble birth. After proper purification by the priests, his remains were kept in state in the great temple of Tojil, the jaguar god. Three days later, with all the honors of his people, his body was cremated in the central court of the temple. A great life had been extinguished. The K'iche nation was in mourning. The harbinger of death had visited the kingdom, ushered in by the Spaniards.

A few days later, the K'iche supreme council named Kakupatak supreme commander of the realm and was instructed to rebuild their defenses. Kakupatak knew that Buluc Chabtan, the god of war, was unhappy with his people. He had the premonition that matters would get worse, more complicated by the presence of the Spaniards. His heart told him they were bloodthirsty and would find an excuse to come back. He had seen the menace in the eyes of the envoys from Alvarado that had visited them a few months before. He was positive about that. He decided he had to prepare the empire for a future invasion.

Chapter 14

After the funeral, once the peace had settled in for few months, Ahau Galel, Prince Tecún, was named Nima (great captain).

Weeks later, Tecún was sitting with his mentor and friend Kakupatak discussing urgent affairs affecting the nation. The war chief said, "Nima, your grandfather was a great man, I miss him terribly. He taught me many useful things, many tactics and discipline, for which I will forever be in his debt. I see in you his greatness and kind heart. I know this is too soon after his death, but we need to discuss strategies to defeat the invaders that came from across the big salty waters. I'm sure they would come back to attacks us, maybe they will even use the K'akchiquels and the Tz'utujils against us."

Tecún and Kakupatak were confused as whether this man Alvarado was indeed the reincarnation of Quetzalcoatl, the white-feathered serpent, who was to reclaim these lands entrusted to them by the gods as prophesied in the great book of the counsel, the book of the mat, their sacred guide, the Popol Vuh. They wondered if the gods were punishing them.

As far as they could remember, the priests always taught the nobility that one day in the future, Quetzalcoatl would come to fulfill this prophesy. Had the time arrived? *They wondered.* They kept asking themselves if they had failed in the tasks entrusted to them. The K'iche people had cared for the land with love and devotion. The crops had been abundant. Ah Mun, the maize god, had been honored as dictated in the revered book. The animals of the forest were respected and venerated. The rivers were kept clean. The temples were well attended and maintained. The faithful attended prayers often and presented their gifts with humility and reverence. Where did they fail? It was a conundrum, a question without an answer to which not even the priests were sure about. Was Jacawitz, their mother goddess unhappy with her children? The questions kept popping up in their minds without respite. Their hearts were heavy with worry. They were baffled!

The rumors of the white men moving against their kingdom kept multiplying.

"*Tata*—father" Tecún said. He grew up with Kakupatak's children and thought of him as his dad. "I wish we could find what their real intentions are. My meetings with the disaffected Choluteca had not shed any light, but as you said, I have a hunch they will soon assault us. These escapees had seen their *caballos* carry the horsemen for great distances. These *micos* [monkeys] also say these animals can outrun our fastest man. These creatures obey them without protestations, with great discipline. You remember when we saw them for the first time; we were so impressed with their beauty and size, though at that time we didn't know they could be used in this manner. Some men assert that this *caballos* can be used during fights against the enemy."

Ixpiyacoc, Tecún's friend, recently named adjutant to Kakupatak, the war chief, intervened in the conversation after getting a nod from his lord, "Nima, Kakupatak, I heard rumors that those furry beasts they call *perros* can attack a man and tear him to ribbons with their powerful jaws, as had been witnessed by some poor runaway slaves [the allied Choluteca had become slaves]. These *perros* can stay silent for hours but attack when their masters order them with silent hand signals. If the foreigners attack us, we need to find a way to defend against those beasts."

Vukub, who had been seconded to Tecún as his aide, intervened in the discussion, "Many Tlaxcalans say that these white *balams* [witches] have long sticks that spew thunder with a great boom, sending metal pellets that can tear a man apart. They are extremely frightened of this fire sticks." He continued, "If we could send some of our warriors to Oaxaca, where the intruders live, maybe we could get more information. I myself offer to lead some volunteers and try to find for sure."

The planning session continued for a few more hours; plans were made, strategies reviewed; some plans were adopted, others were deemed not practical. The plan of Vukub was rehashed and accepted. He would leave in a few days' time.

Late at night, the meeting adjourned. The attendees made plans to keep evaluating and sharing information as it became available. Inexorably, a time bomb was about to go off.

Vukub and a short party of trusted friends left the kingdom, bound for Oaxaca, the seat of Governor Alvarado. Their mission was to get as much military information as was possible. They were mostly worried about the large dogs the Spaniards called *perros*. The party followed the causeway that the merchants used for their trade, seeking refuge in the nearby forest, when another group of people were walking toward them; they didn't want to be discovered. When Vukub's party arrived in Oaxaca, they mingled with the rest of the Indians and kept a safe distance from the Spaniard overseers. The scouts discovered the way the Spaniard soldiers mounted the horses and commanded the dogs with silent signals, safeguarding this information for later delivery to their lord, Tecúm. After several more days of watching the troops, the marauders departed, bound for K'umarkaj.

Chapter 15

NOVEMBER 1523

*P*rince Tecún and his war chief, Kakupatak, after the emissaries from Alvarado had departed, sat down to discuss their attitude and the offer they presented. They both shared a common fear of impending disaster, augmented with the discouraging news filtering from the fallen Aztec empire brought in by the *kaweks* still making the trek between the two metropolises. They brought the alarming notice that Montezuma, the Aztec emperor, was dead, slain by the invading Spaniards, led by Hernán Cortés. Apparently, the deceased Aztec emperor tried to ingratiate himself with the foreigners by offering them gold and jewels, but the Spaniards demanded more and more, and when he finally refused their last extortion, he was rounded up with his wife and family and burned alive.

On seeing this, his son-in-law, Cuauhtémoc, took it upon himself to lead the rebellion, but finally he was also executed in the same horrible manner as his father-in-law, burnt alive.

"Kakupatak," Tecún said, interrupting the reverie, "I'm afraid that war is imminent. I can still feel the arrogance and rudeness of those foreign soldiers who tried to impose their will on us. It was outrageous. I tell you, Tata, I will never willingly submit my people to slavery. I know this is their final goal. We will have to fight to the last man to prevent this from happening." He lent a passion to his words never heard before by his mentor.

Before they separated, Tecún said, "Kakupatak, I want you to inform the lords of the supreme council about the grave danger facing our lands. Arrange a meeting without delay."

"Yes, Nima, my lord, I will proceed at once with your orders," the war chief responded. He then bowed with great respect and left Tecún to carry his instructions. Kakupatak was impressed with the change in Tecún; overnight he had become a leader, sure of himself, still humble but forceful when necessary.

With the prospect of war almost knocking at their door, the city and the provinces became energized. The menace of war had reached a fever pitch. The distant garrisons were reinforced, and the commanders were ordered to be more alert, on the lookout for intruders. The production of arrows and bows were increased. New clubs with studded shards of obsidian were produced in large numbers. Lances and obsidian knives multiplied. Obsidian was used because it was a rock hard as diamond and in great supply in the quarries. The empire was in a war effort.

The attendance to the temples doubled; the priests were offering nonstop prayers asking for deliverance, aimed to placate the wrath of the gods. The priests asked themselves why the gods were angry with them; nobody could understand why that was so. Every citizen was aware of the storm blowing their way, the winds of war gaining gale force, like a hurricane.

Even when the relationships with the K'akchiquels and the Tz'utujils were strained, Tecún decided to send a peace delegation headed by his friend Ixpiyacoc as his personal envoy. His instructions were to make them aware of the common peril they were facing and the need for a united defense. The memory of his slain grandfather was still fresh in his memory, but he tried to forget and was attempting to mend the differences with his neighbors.

A few days later, Ixpiyacoc returned with discouraging news.

"Nima," he addressed his captain and lord, "Acajal, the K'akchiquel lord, and Xahil, the Tz'utujil lord, refused to accept your offer of cooperation. Instead they threatened to complain to their new master, Alvarado that we are preparing to again invade their Kingdom."

Ahau Galel, Prince Tecún, was really disappointed with this open refusal. After a few seconds of reflection, he said, "I'm afraid we are left alone to fight and defeat these invaders. I will have to inform the supreme council of this unwelcome news." He further added, "Ixpiyacoc, my brother, my trusted friend, I thank you for your efforts and for exposing your life in carrying this mission. Go home and rest. I will need your services shortly." He then embraced his friend and left his office looking for his war chief. He had to make him aware of this latest setback.

Vukub and his party returned safe and sound and were soon brought to the presence of Prince Tecún and Kakupatak, the war chief. Vukub informed both of the preparations of the Spaniards and told them that the rumor among the Indians was that Alvarado was getting ready to march against their kingdom. Tecún and Kakupatak were made aware of the way the soldiers used the horses and the dogs. Their worst fears were confirmed. The most alarming news was the way the informants described the weapons that belched fire and death, arms they had never seen before. The two chieftains were perplexed with all this information.

Tecún and Kakupatak, the war chief, were soon engaged in a heated discussion analyzing the urgency of the situation. The sands of time were ebbing inexorably. The horsemen of the apocalypses were getting closer to their beloved kingdom. They both wondered what new disasters awaited them.

Chapter 16

After leaving his palace, Ahau Galel-Tecún, followed by his personal escort, directed his footsteps toward the palace of Ixchel, his fiancée. He missed her intensely. She had become his guiding light in the middle of the darkness. He had not seen her for a few days. He craved her presence. He wanted so much to see that beautiful face ever present in his thoughts. She was so lovely, so fresh, enticing, like a beacon guiding him to safe harbor.

On reaching his destination, Tecún was immediately admitted by the porter and shown into the waiting room. The steward of the house greeted him affectionately, offered him some refreshment, and excused himself, leaving Tecún comfortably seated in one of the best mats to search for his mistress, Princess Ixchel. Almost at once, as if she had been waiting for him in the hall, his fiancée entered the room. With great tenderness she took his hands in hers and brought him close, closer than was permissible, purring softly, "Ahau, my lord, Tecún, my love, my poor sweet love and my heart rejoices with your visit. I have been worried sick for you. I know how busy you are, but I cannot help it, my heart longs for you." She wanted so much to embrace him, to caress his powerful torso; her loins were on fire, demanding more.

She could hardly wait to be his, to share with him her most intimate moments. The days were long and lonely; her nights had become a torture without his presence, her mat was so empty. She really desired him. She so much wanted to kiss his mouth, to caress his neck, his arms, but she could not do that; it would be improper. In her heart she knew Ahau wanted her because she had seen in his eyes the desire, the fire of passion, but years of proper upbringing made them prisoners of the strict Maya social rules. They were nobility; they were expected to set an example for the *kajols*-the serfs.

Ixchel kept gushing, unable to stop; she was on a roll. "Oh, Ahau, I wish I could wash away your burden. So much is riding on your shoulders. My soul bleeds with yours. I know our way of life is in mortal danger and you are trying to prevent this from happening. Do you want to postpone the wedding until this storms passes?" she asked anxiously, holding her breath, eagerly awaiting his response. She was afraid he would take her offer and accept her proposal of postponing the nuptials.

Immediately, without delay, . responded, "No, I wouldn't like to do that. You know my feelings, I want this as much as you do, I want to make you happy. Besides, I cannot be away from you anymore." Tecún kept going, "I know I have not been around as much as I would like, but the days and nights are now so short, so many preparations to be made. When I think everything has been taken care of, another little detail pops up. My mind is overcharged, about to explode. Uncle Kaku, Ixpiyacoc, and Vukub have been of great help, shouldering a lot of work, but still, the final decision is mine. I'm the one responsible for the kingdom."

With a sigh, they finally sat, still holding hands, defying the laws of gravity. Ahau accepted the drink she offered him, and as with any other young couple in love, their conversation soon drifted to more mundane topics, gossip about their friends. Ixchel told Ahau in confidence that her younger sister, K'etzalin, was in love with Ixpiyacoc but that despite her many hints he was oblivious to her enticements, or so it appeared. "Men are so blind," she stated matter-of-factly.

Tecún responded, "I know he likes K'etzalin because he had told me more than once. But even when he is a good hunter and brave like nobody else, when it comes to K'etzalin, he gets tongue-tied and cannot say a word. He gets paralyzed. Maybe next time we are together, we will push them a little. What do you say?"

Ixchel responded, "Absolutely, that's what we would do." In the same breath, she asked Tecún, "What about Vukub? Who should we pair him with?" They discussed many plans; alternatives were explored, but after a while, Tecún started to drift to the problem at hand, unable to concentrate on what Ixchel was saying. Finally, against his wishes, with a heavy heart, after many excuses, Tecún left the company of Ixchel. They promised to see each other soon.

After he left the palace of Ixchel, wandering the streets of his city, Tecún absentmindedly returned the greetings of the people passing by; without realizing it, he found himself at the temple of Tojil, the jaguar god.

His mind kept laboring about the troops' disposition, about the best ways to defend against those *perros* and *caballos*. He kept wondering if he and his lieutenants would fight with honor and determination. Would their foes, the K'akchiquels and Tz'utujils, join forces with the Spaniards in a final act of treachery? Or would they amend their ways and come to realize that their own survival was at stake?

A myriad of questions kept his mind busy. *What do I do?* Rumors of the atrocities inflicted by the dogs unleashed on the enemy intruded his mind. He heard that those creatures were fearsome, implacable and ferocious. So far, the K'iche didn't have any known defense against them. His mind wanted so much to find a way to neutralize those hounds.

Silently he invoked his deity, "Oh, grand Jaguar, give me courage to lead my people, grant me strength and wisdom to face the enemy without flinching. Do not abandon your servant. Oh, god, deliver us from this nightmare." Tecún continued his vigil for some more time. His soul had been refreshed. His mind had been relaxed. His faith had been renewed.

After some more time praying, Tecún left the temple and went back to his palace to again review his plans and those of his war chief, Kakupatak, who had proven cagey and invaluable. The old fox was full of tricks and advice. He had so much experience in matters of war. After all, he had defeated their enemies, the K'akchiquels, not too long ago.

In the morning he would discuss with his aides several ideas that had come to his mind. He made a mental note that he also had to increase the number of troops presently active, which now were not more than four thousand. He would have to recruit soldiers from the distant farms. The K'iche were not a warring nation; they were mostly farmers, with the nobility making the bulk of the actual fighting elements. He had to dispatch orders to that effect as early as possible. Some of the conscripts would have to travel far to reach the city's training grounds. It would be a monumental task to train these men who didn't have any prior warfare experience. Would they come when summoned? Or would they turn a deaf ear to his request even when it would be delivered as a command? Would they leave their farms and families to come to the aid of their capital? So much was uncertain. He didn't know his potential enemy. He had never before met those strange men before the emissaries came. Was he as arrogant as his recently departed soldiers? When he met them, they looked dangerous and vicious. They seemed determined to get, by force if necessary, whatever they wanted. What was the material their hats and chest protector were made of? He was not familiar with that matter. The hat and chest cover were so shiny. He would consult the priests. Maybe they knew, or perhaps some of the *kaweks* would know the name.

He finally succumbed to sleep, a well-deserved respite for his tortured mind. The next few days, maybe months, would be taxing for him and his aides.

Chapter 17

"No, absolutely no," Pedro de Alvarado said to his brother Gómez, who was training the mastiffs preparing them for future action. Apparently, Gómez was not following his instructions. Alvarado continued his diatribe. "Those dogs need to learn to obey silent hand signals. *Me entendeis?* [Do you understand me?] I want to make sure they don't attack our friends the Tlaxcalans and the Choluteca," he went on, saying with a smirk, referring to their allies.

Once his pent-up fury was spent, Alvarado went on his way to keep the supervision of the hand-to-hand combat exercises, prodding the fusiliers to improve their loading time and accuracy. He was also spurring the horsemen to attack with more zest. Most soldiers were veterans of the latest campaigns against the Aztecs up north and the most recent massacres against the indigenous population around the port of Vera Cruz. Many soldiers had drifted to his camp when they learned that he was mounting a new army to invade the new lands to the south of Oaxaca, where Alvarado was the recently appointed governor and where his training grounds were located.

In addition to the Spaniards, two recently vanquished tribes had joined, by force, his army, the Tlaxcalans and the Choluteca, who were now being properly trained in the more efficient European fashion instead of the unruly and disorderly way of fighting they were used to.

Alvarado was still waiting for the answer from Hernán Cortés, his commander, hopefully authorizing him to conduct the invasion of the K'iche kingdom. His impatience was tempered by devoting his empty time to writing poems. His most fervent wish had come true after he improved and mastered his reading and writing aided by one of the priests he had befriended during the many months in campaign, a man called Juan Godinez, a gentleman he found really devoted to God, humble, living in poverty as mandated by his religious order. Grudgingly, he had learned to admire and respect the cleric.

Later on, Pedro de Alvarado went looking for Doña Luisa, his interpreter, to whom he found himself attracted more and more. He had discovered that besides being beautiful, she also possessed a mind singularly acute and bright. Luisa had taught him some basic Maya of which he was so proud because now he could berate his servants in their own language.

When he saw Luisa, Alvarado immediately ordered her, "Luisa, *traedme un chocolate caliente* [bring me some hot cocoa]." Pedro had become addicted to the delicious brew prepared with cacao beans. "Then we will discuss about those savages Quiché who live beyond the Yucatán." He proceeded, "Do you know who they are? Can they fight? What kind of weapons do they possess? Go on; tell me as much as you know. I especially want to know about the man they call Tekún. Who is he? Is he a good warrior? Could he defeat me?"

Luisa was having difficulties in understanding Alvarado's Castilian since he was talking kind of fast, his Extremadura accent getting thicker. She was finally given a chance to answer the barrage of questions directed at her. "Pedro," she answered, emphasizing her by now more familiar tone with him, "they are called the K'iche Empire, they are descendants from the Maya. Basically they are farmers, but their astronomers are well versed in the mysteries of the heavens. They can predict with great confidence events many years into the future. Their forebears go back thousands of Venus cycles, as far as I can remember, close to three thousand cycles. The Haab (long Venus cycle) consists of fifty-two weeks with five additional days considered unworthy to be recorded." She was in flux.

Alvarado was mesmerized with her knowledge, with the information she was spewing; he had a hard time fathoming the fact that these people were probably older than his ancestors.

Luisa continued, "When needed, they can become fierce warriors as proven in the recent wars against the K'akchiquels and the Tz'utujils. Pedro, I do think you might have an advantage over them with your cannons, your *arcabuces* [harquebus], your horses, and those devilish *perros bravos* [the mastiffs]. Your horses can carry your men for many leagues, so they will arrive rested into the battlefield whereas they don't have any animals to carry their burdens; everything has to be carried by the porters, piggyback—*atuto*." She was now wound up. "Even with those handicaps against them, your hands will be full if you decide to invade their *Reino* [realm]." She somehow had guessed the real reason behind his many questions.

Alvarado was pensive, lost in his thoughts. He was dying to march south, but he did not have Cortés's permission as yet. Alvarado didn't want to alienate his protector and friend. He could still remember the tongue-lashing he got from Cortés when, against his orders of not unduly taxing the natives, he had massacred hundreds of rebel natives near Vera Cruz a few years back. His words of reproach still stung his pride.

Pedro de Alvarado was a complex man, sometimes given to extreme acts of kindness, supplanted other times by unimaginable feats of brutality and violence. He was not a malicious man, but he could be cruel, cold and hard, with a streak of viciousness. So in his best interest, against his most fervent wishes, Alvarado decided to wait for Cortés's response.

A few more months were added to the cataclysmic tragedy his actions and avarice would precipitate. He decided to continue with his relentless training of his troops as if he was already proceeding with his military campaign. He would prod his troops to be ready. He would keep enticing them with the promise of wealth. He continued counting the days, ever watchful of the messenger he was so desperately waiting for.

Chapter 18

fter a few more days, the answer from Cortés came in the form of a directive, written in the style of a personal letter but, nevertheless, official in nature and purpose, addressed to Pedro de Alvarado y Contreras, governor of Oaxaca. It read:

Captain Pedro de Alvarado y Contreras, Governor of Oaxaca, by the grace of His Majesty Carlos V, King of Spain

Estimado Pedro [Esteemed Pedro], after a lengthy debate with other officials of the crown and I, it is with great trepidation that I have decided to approve your request to assist our allies the Cachiquels and the Zutujils, whose loyal services to the crown of Spain had been proven beyond any doubt, but I must remind you to avoid, at any cost, I repeat, at any reasonable cost, any armed conflict against the Quiché people whom I still expect to peacefully bring to our side. Therefore, I, as viceroy of New Spain, in the name of Carlos V, our most exalted monarch, with the hope to bring those lost souls to the womb of our holy mother church, order you to include in your expeditionary force two priests of your choosing. Remember that before any hostilities threaten to break out, you are to report such possibility directly to me for consideration and approval of any declaration of war.

New Spain, November 1523
General Hernán Cortés, Viceroy

When Alvarado finished reading the document, a deep and brooding resentment exploded in his mind. With great disdain and fury he crumpled the letter in his hands and threw it to the floor. He then sat down, holding his head with his hands, trying to calm down his inner turmoil, his boiling rage. After a while, once his temper had calmed, he retrieved the directive, called his secretary, and in an imperious manner ordered him to file the missive.

"Manuel, send Doña Luisa to see me immediately," Alvarado instructed the terrified man.

As soon as Luisa entered the office, Alvarado exploded with great alacrity. "The nerve of that man [he was referring to Cortés]. He has approved my request for the journey beyond our borders, but he ordered me, listen, ordered me," Alvarado repeated, "to bring along *dos cuervos* [two crows], not only one, but two sanctimonious clerics to keep an eye on me. That is preposterous. I cannot bear it. He directs me to pacify those savages," Pedro added with venom and disdain in his words. "Well, let me tell you," Alvarado said, pointing a finger at Luisa, "I will not go for it. I flatly refuse to be encumbered with those *buitres* [vultures]. No, no, no."

By now, Luisa, knowing Alvarado's many mood swings, waited patiently for the waters to calm down. She already knew this would happen within a few minutes. Luisa could read him like an open book, her sagacious mind playing with ideas that could benefit her people.

"My lord," she ventured, "calm down, think about it, Cortés had finally accepted your recommendation. Use this opportunity to advance your dreams, pretend to obey his orders but do as you please. After all, what can two priests do when you have all the power? What, will they excommunicate you?" she added with scorn since she had no use for priests. Luisa still worshiped her gods.

At once Luisa knew that Alvarado had come to accept her suggestions when he instructed her to leave shortly and send in Portocarrero and Olid. "Luisa, they need to know about our commission. Go, don't waste any more of my time," Alvarado blurted out.

After a few minutes, his captains were ushered in. Without any niceties or preamble, Alvarado spoke. "Pedro, Cristobal, Cortés has given his permission for our expedition. I would like to leave at the latest in two days. Send scouts to prepare for our arrival into those *lares*," he said, using the Castilian word for *lands*. "Make sure they are familiar with the terrain. I don't want any surprises or delays."

Alvarado kept firing orders on how many men he wanted, how many horses, cannons, *arcabuces (harquebuses)* they were to include in the soon-to-march army. "I want those *mastines* [dogs] ready to move. I will give those savages a taste of my fury and power," he stated with glee.

After dismissing his deputies, Alvarado went back to work, studying the rudimentary maps he had previously acquired; planning his strategy, thinking with longing of the precious treasures his troops would collect for him. He was going to be a wealthy man!

Early next morning, the scouting party left Oaxaca, setting course for the lands lying south, establishing a grueling pace trying to reach their assigned task as soon as was possible and without being detected. They also wanted to be rich and try to buy their freedom to recover at least a little piece of the lands they had lost to the invaders.

The party consisted of twenty experienced trackers with two Spaniards to act as watchdogs. They were to travel light. Their aim was to reach their destination unharmed and report back the number of enemy troops and preparedness, try to flush out or discover the garrisons scattered in the mountains, maybe even try to reach the capital undiscovered. They were a mixed group of Tlaxcalans and Choluteca, commanded by Xicotenga, Doña Luisa's father. One of the Spaniards' liaisons was the sergeant Juan Argueta, one of the new best friends of Alvarado.

Day by day they got closer to their objective, ushering in clouds of destruction, dark forces gathering behind, just waiting to be unleashed on the K'iche kingdom. The scouting party, after traveling night and day, reached the border of the kingdom they were about to invade. The men kept to the side of the causeway and hid themselves when travelers were coming their way. Even when they were incessantly searching for enemy troops, they found none in their way. They kept guessing that maybe the enemy was waiting for them in the nearby forests, but nothing happened. They were almost alone in their forays. Chief Xicotenga suggested to Argueta that they should look for the two renegade caciques Xahil and Acajal, to let them know the intentions of the governor. After some discussion, the Spaniard accepted the suggestion of Xicotenga and set course for Iximche, the capital of the K'akchiquels.

The small party traveled incognito, trying to hide themselves in the near forest, when a party of merchants came. They were invisible in the vegetation bordering the causeway. After this almost casual encounter, they only made brief stops to eat few pieces of dried meat complemented with fruits and vegetables. Alvarado had instructed them not to kindle any fires, afraid that the smoke would attract attention.

Juan Argueta, despite his age and recent inactivity, was able to keep up with the Indian guides, though he was riding his horse. But he kept spurring his charges mercilessly. He knew that his fortune depended on carrying this mission successfully. Besides, he owed Alvarado an immense debt of gratitude after he rescued him from his depression way back in Cádiz. Since then, Argueta became his lapdog, willing to carry out the most absurd of orders as far as they came from the lips of his idol. He worshiped his master blindly. After a few miles of hard march, the column was surprised by a band of K'iche scouts, and three intruders were taken as prisoners. The rest of the group were able to escape capture and retreated the way they had come. They had been discovered!

Chapter 19

Moving with haste down the halls of Tecún's palace was Chilam Kinich, captain of the imperial guard. He was looking for his lord, Prince Ahau Galel-Tecún. He had alarming news to communicate. He had to warn his principal without delay.

After taking a few shortcuts, Kinich reached the chambers of the Lord Chancellor, Yum Kaax Ik. Once the chancellor was awoken, Kinich was brought to his presence. The captain, after taking a short breath to steady his voice, addressed him, "Lord Chancellor, my apologies for interrupting your sleep at this hour, but the news I have cannot wait." He then waited permission from the official to proceed. The Lord Chancellor, still not fully awake, spat his words with anger, "Captain Kinich, do you realize it is two in the morning? Since by now I'm fully awake, tell me what is so alarming that cannot wait a few more hours?"

With great detail, Captain Kinich told his story. On hearing it, Yum Kaax Ik, the chancellor, was taken aback by these alarming tidings. Without waiting for the captain to follow him, he took off at great speed for his overweight body in search of his prince, Tecún, whose lodgings were a short walk away in the north wing of the palace. Upon reaching the premises, Yum Kaax informed the soldier guarding Tecún's antechamber that he had to see the prince at once, ordering the guard to take him to his lord's chambers.

By now Tecún already was fully awake and immediately came out, wondering what could be wrong. When he saw Yum Kaax, his heart skipped a beat; Tecún knew that Yum Kaax, despite his demeanor, was not given to false alarms. Tecún promptly asked Yum, "Lord Chancellor, what is the reason for this interruption?"

Yum, in a vacillating voice, said, directing his eyes to the man accompanying him, "My prince, Captain Kinich has news that you have to hear now, something that cannot wait any longer."

Tecún, without a moment's hesitation, ordered the captain to speak.

"My lord, today several Tlaxcalans spies were captured near the city's outer skirts." He made a brief pause and continued. "Under duress, they have confessed that a great army in Oaxaca is getting ready to march against us. These *micos* state that this force is led by a pale, tall man with eyes the color of the sky, his hair golden as our maize. They call him Tonatiuh [the sun]. They swear this man is a god, the messenger of Quetzalcoatl, sent by the heavens from across the big waters to reclaim in his name our kingdom, that for many centuries was entrusted to us by K'uq'matz, our white-feathered serpent," the captain concluded, waiting for instructions from his prince.

On hearing this unwanted news, Ahau Galel-Tecún shivered. He knew that the Popol Vuh, the sacred book of the counsel, had prophesied the return of the white-feathered serpent, K'uq'matz. Even when this event had been known and been waited for by his people for centuries, he could not believe this would happen so soon or in his lifetime. He urged Kinich to continue.

"My lord, these men say that the warriors with this man, they call *soldados* [soldiers], carry with them a long tube that belches fire with a great noise and can kill any men it strikes." Kinich was afraid to continue with more bad news, but with encouragement from his prince, he resumed his report. "Some of these *soldados* climb on top of those big, furry animals they call *caballos* and with great ease direct these creatures to trot and carry them wherever they want to go. The spies say that these beasts can run really fast and can outrun our fastest men." A brief pause ensued.

"Go on, I know there is more," Tecún said.

"The foreigner also has those mean-looking, grisly creatures they call *perros* that can attack with great speed and fury. These beasts can tear a man to pieces with their powerful *jetas* [jaws]," Kinich concluded uneasily, trembling, quite unusual for the captain, waiting for his lord's instructions.

Ahau-Tecún was mystified by this news. Even when the Maya-K'iche people were familiar with and had small dogs, they had never before seen these large creatures and didn't know the havoc they could wreak.

A curious and inexplicable uneasiness crept along Tecún's spine, sending his mind into overdrive; the moment he dreaded had arrived, way too soon. They were not yet ready.

Tecún spoke, "Yum, notify Kakupatak about our discussion, assemble the supreme council this morning, they need to hear these terrible reports. Notify each member of the council by special messenger, I want everyone to be present. We need to make decisions that cannot wait."

After Tecún showed his appreciation for his prompt thinking and the delivery of the news, Captain Kinich was dismissed with instructions to notify his friends Ixpiyacoc and Vukub that they were expected to be present at the meeting as befitting their noble ranks and as being adjutants to him and the war chief. Vukub, on his return from his foray into Oaxaca had told Tecún some of this news, but even so, he was surprised to learn that the enemy was getting ready to march on to his kingdom.

Prince Tecún gave a few more pertinent instructions to his chancellor, Yum Kaax, who soon departed to prepare the next steps in the drama that would unfold within a few more weeks. Yum was afraid, really afraid. He wondered what would happen with the kingdom he had so relentlessly worked to keep and build up. He had been so diligent in making changes to the social and political infrastructure. The city had become a great enclave in the mountains. The temples were magnificent. Their farms were producing incredibly large crops. The realm had prospered under his helm despite the wars against his enemies. What was he to do? Could he do more to prevent any catastrophe? He dispatched the messengers to summon the lords to the fateful meeting.

Chapter 20

DECEMBER 1523

With great pomp and a lot of shouting, Pedro de Alvarado y Contreras, governor of Oaxaca, riding his magnificent Andalusian mare, Corazón, left town. He was resplendent in his polished breastplate and helmet, his beard recently trimmed and reshaped.

His newly designed pennant was proudly carried by Juan Argueta, riding a few meters behind his captain. The few Spaniards left in charge of the town were lamenting about not being part of the expedition, but they consoled themselves thinking that somebody had to man the defenses of the place, even when there was not too much to guard.

The army Alvarado commanded was bound for K'umarkaj, the capital of the Maya-K'iche kingdom, many leagues south of his departure point. Alvarado was full of confidence, dreams of glory and the possibility of acquiring many tons of gold, with some silver thrown in to complement his insatiable greed.

The invading force included the following:

120 mounted soldiers with pike, sword, helmet and breastplate
130 *ballesteros* (crossbowmen)
170 foot soldiers
30 fusiliers equipped with harquebuses
200 Tlaxcala indians under their cacique, Xicotenga
100 Choluteca Indians
The contingent was complemented with the following:
40 replacement horses
50 mules

4 small cannons
20 mean-looking mastiffs, including Valor, Alvarado's dog, and
  Amigo, Rodrigo Sosa's dog

Alvarado had also enrolled in the mission his brothers Gómez, Gonzalo, and Jorge, as well as his cousin and confidant Rodrigo Sosa. Embedded in the soldiery were Alvarado's trusted captains Pedro Portocarrero and Cristobal Olid.

Along with these men, Alvarado had pressed again into service that obscure sergeant named Juan Argueta, a soldier of fortune that eventually would change the course of history in the conquest of the Maya kingdom of the K'iche and the fate of the last Maya prince, Ahau Galel, Tecún. He also begged his two cleric friends Juan Godinez and Juan Diaz to accompany the caravan, using the enticement of saving the souls of the aborigines they were about to conquer.

The causeway the troops were traveling was wide, but it was not designed to handle that much traffic, let alone so many men, animals and materiel together.

The Tlaxcalans and Choluteca natives, loaded with heavy burdens, like mules, were walking with great difficulty, trying to avoid the swamps and the thick vegetation bordering the road. They were silently lamenting their misfortune after they were made slaves by the conquering Spaniards, who constantly abused not only them but also their wives and daughters, using those poor wretched creatures as sex slaves or do home labor and any other tasks they devised to keep them occupied. The vanquished people were also forced to learn the Catholic faith and were savagely punished when they were discovered worshipping their idols.

The foreign soldiers were also complaining of the heat, the mosquitoes, the high humidity, the serpents lurking in the brushes, and any other obstacle, real or imagined. They were not used to this climate, but they were partially lucky since the indians were carrying all their equipment but their swords and helmets, which with the sun became like small portable furnaces, making them sweat like peons.

The sun was merciless, blistering. The men were sweating profusely, making the dust kicked by the horses and mules ahead to stick to their hair, face, neck, back, loins, every little crevice of their bodies. The soldiers were choking despite covering their mouths with handkerchiefs used like bandanas, but they kept moving forward, shuffling their feet, advancing relentlessly, spurred by the prospect of fabled riches to be plundered from the heathens toward whom they were moving like a cloud of death and destruction.

It was every soldier's dream to become rich and return to their native land with honors and a new standing in the pecking order of his hometown. Maybe marry one of the rich girls they had kept in their memory as something that was unattainable if they were poor. They would become the new nobility, the reaper of adulation, perks, and almost an unending array of benefits.

Walking at the side of Alvarado, holding to one of his stirrups, was Doña Luisa, assisted by several Indian women who were expected to cook, wash the garments of the soldiers, and tend to other needs of the troops. Alvarado had offered Luisa a tame mare to ride, but she refused the offer. Luisa was deathly afraid of the furry beasts despite many reassurances from many well-intentioned Spaniards, Alvarado included.

Alvarado had fallen hard for Doña Luisa. The excuse he used in justifying her coming was that she would serve as his counselor and interpreter besides her other role as his concubine. The princess had wormed her way into Pedro's heart and now enjoyed many privileges only accorded to Spaniards. She reasoned that in using these gifts, she could influence Alvarado's thinking and intercede in the name of his people, although, more and more, she was losing her heart to the blond foreigner.

Way back, in the background were the women pressed into involuntary service, breathing the dust raised by the caravan, their naked torsos caked with sticky dirt, carrying on their heads the utensils for cooking. They marched silently, by now used to the abuses of their new bosses, afraid to displease them. Nobody paid attention to them; they were expendable, passed like objects from master to master, like ghosts, used and discarded at pleasure.

Chapter 21

A small group of K'iche *kaweks* en route to Oaxaca saw in the distance a cloud of dust. Then suddenly, like an apparition from Xibalbá (hell), surging from the blur, a group of horsemen approached at full speed, like bolts, ethereal. The merchants, without a second's hesitation, took off, fast disappearing in the underbrush bordering the causeway.

The traders were lucky because the riders in their haste did not take notice of their presence nor ordered the mastiffs by their side to attack them. Concealed in the bush, the *kaweks* watched the huge horses and the small brutes trotting by their side. They wondered if such beasts were monsters that escaped from the netherworld. After the caravan passed, the merchants decided to return to their land and warn the royal families. They were so afraid of the enormous force marching south, possibly toward their homeland.

Oblivious to this small incident, Pedro de Alvarado kept his pace, riding his noble mare, Corazón, with his loyal mastiff, Valor, running at the other side, opposite Doña Luisa.

Even when the dog was busy chasing butterflies, birds, and any other animal in his path; his eyes did not miss much. Valor was always alert, on guard, only waiting for his master's orders. The hound had grown into a ferocious beast with a shiny black pelt, liquid brown eyes, large paws, and extremely powerful jaws capable of crushing the bones of any unfortunate victim that crossed his path. He was a menacing sight. A well honed machine of destruction, a brute.

Alvarado's long blondish tresses were plastered to his face, his neck; he was sweating buckets, drenched. His pale skin was an intense red, not used to the inclement weather and the punishing sun. His lips were dry and cracked with dust, but despite his discomfort, he kept urging his troops to move on.

"*Diablos, cuando acabará esta tortura? Me siento como en el infierno.* [The devil when will this torture end? I feel as if I'm in hell]," Alvarado voiced to no one in particular, but Doña Luisa, walking by his side, smiled lopsidedly. She loved to see his delicate skin suffer. At least that gave her some small comfort.

For his part, Gonzalo, Alvarado's oldest brother, was bitching nonstop, driving his fellow travelers crazy with his whining. "Pedrito," he said, using Alvarado's infancy name, "why did you bring us to this godforsaken place? We were doing fine in Oaxaca, with plenty of food, wine, and sometimes the company of a woman [he meant an Indian slave]." The litany continued for miles, with some soldiers catcalling back and forth, exchanging insults, barbs, threats, and jokes.

The leagues kept piling on, relentlessly, slowly getting them closer and closer to their final destination.

On the sixth-of December 1523, the invading army crossed the imaginary border at a site called Charual. The spot was nothing but another dot lost in their rudimentary maps provided by Cortés and improved by Alvarado's diligence. The men guiding them were also somehow familiar with the area.

Doña Luisa de Xicotencalt was also aware of the crossing, silently walking beside Alvarado's mare, feeling the earth under her feet as she desired, relishing the relative freedom she enjoyed under her master. Besides, she was used at walking long distances.

After a few miles, Luisa spoke, "My lord, you know that recently we crossed the border, and we are now in the land of the K'iche people. Remember, their king don't want you or any of your soldiers in his kingdom. Tekún was clear in his orders when he dismissed Pedro and Cristobal after the failed 'peace offering you made," she admonished Alvarado.

"*Si, Luisa, lo entiendo. Sé que ahora estamos en territorio enemigo.* [Yes, Luisa, I understand. We are now in enemy territory.] But we need to keep going. Don't forget I promised to punish those savages. I will alert the men to be more vigilant. Thank you for your advice," Alvarado closed the discussion.

The march continued, the soldiers keeping pace, walking in silence, with occasional catcalls. They were tired, hungry, hot, and miserable. They longed for rest and food.

After the blistering swamps of the Yucatán, the terrain started to change. The majestic cedar and oak trees were replaced by tall, gigantic pines, abundant grass, and game animals. The weather became balmier, more pleasant, with a slight cool breeze, but the nights turned colder, sometimes with freezing temperatures at night for which they had not prepared with appropriate garments. Some enterprising men were using the saddle blankets to keep the cold out. The indians had to huddle together to keep from freezing. The mornings were resplendent, and a pleasant piney scent permeated the air. The travelers were so gratified for the change in temperature and the breathtaking scenery. Their mood had changed.

After many miles inland, the trekkers found an immense river with deep rapids, crystalline water, inviting, beckoning the weary travelers who like children, soldiers and Indian porters, made a mad dash for the stream, savoring the fresh, sweet water, cavorting with shouts of joy. The horses drank enormous amounts of the precious liquid until their bellies ached with pleasure.

The mastiffs, more cautious of the waters, kept their distance from the current but finally succumbed to the temptation and went into the river, splashing the waters with their enormous paws, making ripples as they swam contentedly.

After a short, well-deserved respite, Alvarado ordered to resume the march. They had to find a shallow place to cross the raging waters since no bridge was found that could support the weight of so many men, horses, mules, cannons, and war materiel. After a few more hours, the column found a suitable place to cross the river. The trek across happened without a mishap.

Once on the other side, they found that the road kept ascending, became narrower, up immense mountains, with deep ravines, some reaching down hundreds of meters. The landscape was imposing but treacherous, making the advance of the horses and mules extremely difficult. The beasts, in some stretches, had to be unloaded because they had a hard time negotiating the loose rocks. Even moving with extreme caution, some animals fell to the void, sometimes carrying with them their keepers, who went down screaming, their cries reverberating in the solitary gorges.

The porters were given more loads to carry on their backs. The cannons and the cannonballs were especially heavy and awkward to transport, many times needing four or six people to move them. It was a nightmare, but the men persisted in the effort.

Alvarado was merciless in pushing his troops, cajoling, threatening, enticing them with the promise of gold, jade and riches beyond their wildest dreams. Greed became a powerful engine. The prospect of glory turned into a goddess calling them. All of them wanted to be rich, powerful and famous.

The slave porters only made silent gestures of despair; they were condemned to a life of eternal servitude or to be killed by the K'iche people. Their lives were worth nothing! They felt being punished for their alliance with these devils. The advance continued unchallenged. The invaders hadn't found any enemy soldiers. Maybe they didn't exist. Perhaps all was a trick of Xicotenga, the Tlaxcala cacique.

Chapter 22

The supreme council of the lords of the K'iche kingdom assembled in the vast hall of the Guardians of the Sacred Book, the Popol Wuj (Vuh), located in the immense temple dedicated to Q'uq'umatz, the white-feathered serpent, the founder and protector of the realm. The auditorium could easily accommodate up to five hundred guests. The hall was reserved for special meetings involving momentous decisions or the security of the K'iche Empire.

The attendees were seated in luxurious mats of brilliant colors, weaved from plump cotton and stuffed with soft bird feathers. The seating was done according to lineage, rank, and seniority, with the more experienced elders sitting closer to the center of the precinct, each one representing the four royal families.

The proceedings were opened by the supreme priest, Ah Pun Kisin; his invocation was addressed to the patron goddess, Awilix.

Ah Pun Kisin, with great reverence spoke in a deep, sonorous voice, "Our mother of the earth, creator of life, giver of comfort, soul of the maize, star of the heavens, keeper of our traditions, hear our humble plea, give us wisdom to follow the precepts of the sacred book, the Wuj. Open our hearts and minds to accept the second coming of our god Q'uq'umatz, who has returned to earth to reclaim from us his lands that he entrusted to us many centuries ago. Grant us our reward for being good stewards and servants. Oh, sweet Mother, enlighten our minds." He took a brief pause and continued, "Make our eyes sharp as those of our sacred bird quetzal, turn our thoughts toward your divine mercy to steady our hearts to give back to Tonatiuh, your messenger, all the lands and blessings many centuries before you gave us." Once the offering was closed, Ah Pun Kisin sat down.

A great hush descended on the auditorium; all present were praying for wisdom, for guidance to choose the correct path in these trying times.

Nobody wanted to make a terrible mistake. The reverie was broken when Ahau Kinich, the present ruler of the kingdom, stood up, commencing his appeal, "My lords, this foreigner has arrived at our doorstep bringing with him our enemies, the K'akchiquels and the Tz'utujils, now his *kajols*." He proceeded, "The merchants en route to Oaxaca encountered them on the road leading to our city. They saw many of those huge beasts they call *caballos*, like the ones we saw when the foreigners came to our metropolis. As most of you know, the invaders used them against the Aztecs with deadly results, the horsemen using their lances and swords to annihilate their warriors."

He went on to describe all the horrors visited on those neighbors to the north. He emphasized that that nation was reduced to tinder when their rulers tried to oppose their offers. He continued, "We could not accept the offer of alliance their lord presented us because he was going to enslave our people, abuse our women, disrespect our gods, and destroy our temples."

He took a short pause and reassumed his peroration, "Our neighbors the Tlaxcalans and Choluteca describe him as Tonatiuh, the sun. They say he is our revered white-feathered serpent, Quetzalcoatl, but the foreigner has no mercy, he mistreats his own people and even worse, the ones he has conquered, with more cruelty, punishes them for the smallest infractions. I say he is not Q'uq'umatz. The question to you, lords, is, do we welcome him as the representative of our god or do we oppose him and fight to defend our lands?"

Kinich was now on a roll. He kept going, "The astronomers have sighted Venus, the morning star, closer to the earth. The priests affirm that this closeness will bring with her great suffering for our people. I say we fight or we perish in the attempt defending our freedom, our lands, our own way of life." His harangue continued for more than two hours. The audience was spellbound by his words, worried, at times expressing approval, other times murmuring dissent. He finally sat, leaving the air thick with despair, gripping their very hearts, the tempers simmering to a boiling frenzy, quite unusual for such a reserved people. Most were debating the best way to approach the problem they were facing; some were afraid of committing themselves to an action they might regret later on.

The next speaker to stand was the war chief, Kakupatak. All eyes were glued on him, anxiously watching his every move, trying to gauge his body language. His opinion was highly respected, and he was considered the closest representative of the deceased great king Don K'iqab. His demeanor, utterly somber, his words tempered by the brief memory of visualizing those magnificent horses and the two large dogs that he saw during the visit of the barbarians.

He finally spoke, "My lords, we captured several spies of the white man they call Tonatiuh. His real name is Pedro de Alvarado, and he comes from across the big salty lake. As Quetzalcoatl, his hair is yellow, like our sacred maize. His eyes are the color of the sky, but they are described as hard, cold, calculating. His heart is hard as obsidian, cruel with his servants, as was witnessed by the sons and daughters of the emperor Montezuma, who was painfully slain by this man's superior, a man named Cortés. I have a witness that states this monarch was burned alive when he refused to give him more gold. The fate of his son-in-law, Cuauhtémoc, was equally cruel and unjustified when he opposed his desire for more treasure."

Kakupatak continued with his speech, "This man Alvarado has no religion and laughs at their priests. His only god is gold." After a short pause, he finally said, "I propose our prince, Ahau Galel, heir to the throne, from the noble house of Tekún, to be our new Nima Rajpop Achij. As you well know, I saw him born; I have witnessed his coming of age to become a brave fighter, capable, dependable, smart, and even tempered. His skills with the lance, the bow and arrows, as well as with the *honda* are unsurpassed. I knew his father and fought alongside his grandfather Don K'iqab, who gave his life protecting our values and our independence. Ahau has proved beyond any doubt that he is capable of leading our nation to victory, to defeat those foreigners." He sat down, exhausted, waiting with hope and apprehension the decision of the council.

Ahau Galel, Tecún, sitting in the hall, not too close to the center but not too far as to become invisible, was surprised to hear his nomination by Kakupatak, his friend, his mentor, his father figure. He was overwhelmed with his trust and the prospect of becoming the defender of his country. He was so young! Only twenty-four Venus cycles, he thought. His mind was in overdrive; so many things to do if he was chosen, hundreds of details to consider; plans for the defense of the homeland to be drawn and executed in a short time.

The arguments continued. Many more members expressed their opinions, some of them appealing for appeasement and negotiations while others were clamoring for war.

Finally, the assembly voted. The proponents of defending the homeland won the day. A state of war was declared. The K'iche nation was about to face its greatest challenge.

By overwhelming majority, unopposed, Ahau Galel, Tecún, was elected Nima Rajpop Achij (Great Captain) General Tecúm, grandson of the K'iche king Don K'iqab.

After a while, the great hall emptied swiftly, with most of the participants going back to their homes.

Kakupatak, the war chief, Nima Rajpop Achij, and his lifelong friends Ixpiyacoc and Vukub remained on the premises, discussing their next moves in this lethal chess game. They already knew that the invading army had crossed their borders unimpeded. They had been caught unawares. Nobody thought the foreigners would come so soon; they were appalled at knowing that many Tlaxcalans and Choluteca had joined the invader, following, without knowing, the same path that the K'akchiquels and Tz'utujils had elected to follow to ally themselves with the foreigner, betraying their own people.

Dark clouds of gloom were gathering, obscuring the skies. Tecúm wondered if his leadership would safeguard his kingdom. Hard times were looming ahead. Tecún's mind kept mulling the prophecies the priests had foretold, going as far as 2012 in the future by the calendar of the invaders, the year 3138 in the Haab, the long Maya calendar. Were the sages correct in their predictions?

What would happen if he failed his people? What would be the fate of Ixchel, his lovely fiancée? What about her *nana*, Ixmucané, whom he had come to love as his real mother? K'etzalin, his future sister-in-law, also intruded his thoughts. What a monumental task he was facing!

They had so little time to prepare their defenses. The invaders were already on the march, getting closer, their advance so far unchallenged. What was he to do to oppose these intruders? He was untested in battle, though he knew that he was capable of fighting, but would his courage be enough to defeat the advancing menace? He and Kakupatak would have to speed the preparations to repel the foreign army and the mongrels K'akchiquels and Tz'utujils. Would the Tlaxcalans and Choluteca fight along the Spaniards, or would they come to their side? All was an open question. He would meet with his adviser and come up with a plan, a plan that would give them victory. Tecúm was praying for a miracle or at least a favorable sign from the heavens that they would be victorious. He would have to dispatch scouts to assess the proximity of the enemy troops. Would it be a good strategy to fight in the forests, which they knew so well? The problem was that he didn't have a regular army with properly trained soldiers for guerrilla warfare.

Chapter 23

After a day's long march, the invading Spaniard army reached a plateau with a small stream running through it. Since the night was fast approaching, Alvarado decided to set up camp for the evening for a well-deserved rest. The troops were exhausted. The slaves were beyond tired. They could barely continue walking. Some were almost dragging their heavy burdens.

Alvarado instructed his brother Gómez to supervise the guards and post them to cover all corners of the camp to prevent any surprise attacks. I don't trust these Quiché. For all I know, they could now be lurking in the woods. He further said, referring to one of his captains, Cristobal Olid, "Cristobal, take with you a few soldiers and some Indians and get us some meat for dinner. Bring with you two mastiffs and keep your eyes peeled open. I don't want any sneaky attack."

Alvarado kept firing orders until he was satisfied that all possible contingencies were covered. He was anxious. So far they had not been discovered, but their luck could not hold forever, he thought with yearning. Some of the Tlaxcalans were thinking about escaping, but they were extremely afraid to even try because of the mastiffs. They knew that if they were caught running away, it meant severe punishment, even death at the jaws of those monsters of prey. No way would they make any attempt. Their Spaniard masters had turned to be brutal in punishing the least deviation, eager with the whip. The Tlaxcalans missed the relative freedom they had enjoyed under their cacique. They lamented the decision of Xicotenga to ally them with these barbarians. The insult was made worse when Xicotenga gave his most beautiful daughter to Hernán Cortés, and he, disregarding her royal lineage, like an object, gave her to Pedro de Alvarado. They consoled themselves that at least Don Pedro, as they called him, showed more consideration and seemed to respect her.

These men were sure the day of reckoning was fast approaching. If for any chance they were lucky enough to escape undetected, the trek back home was long and treacherous; then what? Going to the K'akchiquels, the new puppets of the Spaniards, was out of the question because these idiots would turn them in. They were waiting for some food to be thrown at them. Finally, once the mastiffs were fed, the natives got the last scraps of food; after all, their lives were less important that the dogs! They were nothing but invisible creatures used at the whim of their conquerors.

Darkness soon descended on the camp, bringing with her alien noises, fretful slumber; the aggressors were afraid of being taken by the owners of these forests. Their simple minds were so full of superstitions. It would be a long night. God only knew what was hiding in the shadows. Even the veteran soldiers were not used to the solitary woods. They were always afraid of the darkness. The lands they came from were for the most part flat, with different or no vegetation at all.

Alvarado, in his paranoia, had ordered that the kindling of fires was kept to a minimum, barely enough to cook the meat that the hunters were able to gather before, but not big enough to take the chill of the night. Another cold and miserable night!

As the night descended, the big predators started their night symphony of growling. The soldiers lamented that they could not play the few guitars they brought along, let alone sing. They had to talk in whispers, which was kind of silly since probably no enemy was nearby, or so they hoped.

Chapter 24

"What? You are telling me that two of your party of trackers was captured?" Alvarado roared at Sergeant Juan Urrea, one of the two Spaniards that had headed the advance party to the capital of K'umarkaj trying to get more information for his master, Alvarado, who couldn't believe the ineptitude of these people. They had been discovered. Now he had to speed up his plans; otherwise, he would not be able to conquer those pesky K'iche. Alvarado dismissed the returning party and went back to review his plans; in the meantime, he would try to get some rest. The camp was soon closed for the long night.

During one of the strategy planning sessions, Nima Rajpop, Tecúm, had ordered a group of men commanded by his friend Vukub to infiltrate behind the enemy lines to obtain as much intelligence as was feasible regarding the capabilities of the invaders, try, if possible, kill as many men, horses, and dogs as they could. Before he was ordered by his commander, Vukub had volunteered to lead these marauders. Now, he and his men were approaching downwind from the camp. Vukub and his party of intruders could hear low voices as if spoken in hushed tones.

He could not understand what the voices were saying. It was a language he had not heard before; it sounded soft, musical, despite the rough undertones. The voices sounded similar to the one the Spaniards that visited his capital spoke among them, but he was not completely sure. Could it be that the army they were warned about was so close to his capital? he wondered.

The K'iche were not used to night fighting and were wondering if the foreign invaders fought at night. Could their clear eyes see in the dark? Or were they also blind to the demons hiding in the forests? Were the *caballos* and *perros* able to see in the darkness? Could the dogs smell their presence?

Vukub was a cautious man; after all, he had survived many encounters with the K'akchiquels and the Zutujils, but these *balams, brujos* were different. His party had themselves smeared with castor oil (ricin) trying to go undetected, as if they were hunting for deer. They were immobile, like trees. The only movement was from their eyes, probing for weak spots in the enemy camp.

After some more time watching the foreigners, Vukub decided to rest for the night. In the morning, they would again continue shadowing their prey, waiting for an opportunity to attack them.

No fire was lit. They ate in silence *ticucos* (corn cakes) and *cecina* (dried meat). Previously they had filled their *tecomates* (empty gourds) with freshwater from a nearby creek. No words were exchanged. They communicated with silent signals.

A few hours later, a strange noise awoke Vukub, a disturbance he could not identify; it sounded like the purr of the jaguars but not quite. He was intrigued. Then, with alarm he soon realized the commotion was caused by the growling of the mastiffs that were approaching silently. Without hesitation, Vukub and his men got promptly to their feet, on guard, not moving, trying to go undetected, ready to defend themselves against any threat.

After a while, the turmoil subsided, and they were able to resume their vigil though they were weary. The beasts had not detected them. The use of the castor oil had neutralized the hounds' noses.

In the morning, with the sun still barely showing his face in the horizon, the army started to wake up and shortly resumed the march, with Vukub and his party still tailing them, matching their steps, one by one, like a sinister ballet, gliding with great stealth. For many miles the watch continued.

Some of Vukub's men were following a small detachment of two Spaniards and several indians who were probably searching for game. The rest of his force continued following the main body of the army.

Suddenly, out of nowhere, a huge mastiff materialized among the group of trackers, clamping the leg of one of Vukub's men who, taken by complete surprise, howled in pain; the pressure of the jaws of the monster was unbearable, excruciating, the blood draining down the length of the leg of the victim until finally a great chunk of flesh and bone came loose, trapped in the teeth of the mastiff. Holding his mauled leg, the man collapsed to the ground, screaming with all his might.

Instantaneously a loud boom was heard, and Vukub saw, from a distance, another man from his party grab his chest, blood flowing in torrents through his fingers. The poor man could not understand what was happening to him, why he was dying.

Vukub's party had been discovered by the mastiffs that had crept silently, attacking his men savagely. It was their first direct encounter with these ghastly beasts, an animal of these proportions unknown to them until now.

Vukub also wondered what that thunder that killed his warrior was. He could not believe what his eyes had witnessed. How was it possible for these men to have acquired such incredible firepower? Did they have a pact with Xibalbá, the ruler god of the underworld?

On seeing his party discovered and attacked in this savage way, Vukub ordered his men to run for their lives, to save themselves; his first priority became to alert his lord, Tecúm, his Nima Rajpop Achij, about the imminent danger moving their way.

His plan of surprising the enemy had failed; those furry demons had surprised them. He had never seen that long stick with the big mouth that belched fire and death. Was Buluc, one of the rulers of the underworld in league with these devils? He asked himself.

For a while his fleeing party used the creek for concealment, trying to outdistance the pursuers. The chase went on for some time until the followers gave up, when the prowlers became lost in the dense wooded area, becoming part of the forest. The pursuers realized with dismay that the trees were so close one to each other making it hard to see where their prey was headed. Despite the dense forest, the mastiffs tried to move through the trees but were prevented from doing so when the handlers were unable to negotiate the narrow paths. With loud imprecations, the pursuers abandoned the chase and started back to their lines. The mastiffs were not happy; they had been deprived of a succulent feast. They were growling loudly, showing their discontent.

The soldiers were still marveling at the stealth with which the savages had approached their camp. "*Tal vez son brujos y pueden ocultarse en la selva* [maybe they are sorcerers and can hide in the forest]," some soldiers expressed. The chasers were also afraid of being ambushed; they had no knowledge of the capabilities of the enemy. The sergeant in charge of the party realized with glee that they had so far been lucky to escape unharmed. He silently thanked his God for the presence of the mastiffs and the comfort of their firearms. Now he was sure the savages had never seen such weapons. He filed this information in his mind, which he later would pass to his superior, Governor Alvarado. Maybe he would even be rewarded instead of being punished.

Chapter 25

The fugitives, using their knowledge of the bushes, masked their trail by walking for some distance on rhubarb plants, hoping that the tangy scent released by the crushed leaves would confuse the mastiffs. After a few more minutes, the party, still keeping a brisk pace, went waddling into the stream.

They were shamefaced because they had left behind some of their wounded comrades. Vukub was especially mortified. How would he explain to his lord the abandonment of his injured soldiers? Though he knew that one of them was already dead, killed by the thunder spewed by the wide mouth of the long stick the Spanish soldier was firing. The other man was bleeding so much from his mutilated leg that he by now was probably dead.

Vukub kept replaying in his mind the horrible hole opened in the chest of the victim when the fire hit. He had never seen so much blood; he could not comprehend the gruesome picture. He had to reach his lines and tell his lord, Tecúm, of this frightening weapon. What was it? How could the Spaniard soldiers have mastered to harness the power of fire in a stick?

How was it possible? Were they shamans, *brujos*?

After a few more days of forced march, the runaway party reached a friendly garrison from which they could, in the distance, see the city of Q'umarkaj, their final destination. The commander of the garrison had welcomed the escapees with exclamations of joy for their miraculous escape. He realized that the men were famished, thirsty, and dead tired. The food they were provided was wolfed down in mere seconds. They hadn't eaten in more than two days.

Once his men were fed and rested, Vukub gave an account of their lucky getaway; he did not omit any details. He needed to empty his mind of this terrible encounter. Kaibil, the commander of the post, after hearing the details, dispatched a courier with written notes of the incident to warn his Nima Rajpop Achij of the grave danger they were about to face. The messenger was properly warned about the nasty mastiffs.

Early next day, after thanking and wishing his friend Kaibil good luck, Vukub and his men started the trek back to the capital. His most urgent desire was to speak with his Nima, Tecúm, and warn him of the mortal danger they would have to face.

Forcing the pace, after two more days of running, the escaped group reached the palace of Tecúm, the Nima Rajpop Achij. Without delay, on seeing them, the captain of the imperial guard, Chilam Kinich took them to see their commander.

When the group entered the sanctum, Tecúm and Kakupatak, the war chief, were engrossed in a session of strategy. Both men stared with surprise and relief at the newcomers, happy to see them back, hoping against hope to dispel the terrible news the courier had brought the previous day.

Ahau Galel, Tecúm, showed relief to see his friend Vukub back, safe for the time being. He embraced him with great affection and exclaimed, "Well done, my brother, I welcome you and your men with great joy. We were worried for you because so many days went by with no news from your party. Have a seat, tell us again what happened."

Vukub, after bowing respectfully, addressed his commander, "Nima, we discovered the foreign invaders in league with some traitorous K'akchiquels acting as their guides." He took a brief respite, gathered his thoughts, and continued, "The white men have this powerful stick that spews fire. One of my men was ripped to shreds by this loud boom. His chest was split, completely open, like a watermelon hit by thunder. He died bleeding copiously. Another man was attacked by one of those animals they call *perro*. The monster completely took his leg apart with his powerful jaws. It was ghastly.

"My lord, I'm ashamed because we ran. I could not save the men and abandoned them to the aggressors. I beg your forgiveness for my cowardice. I don't deserve to lead my men anymore." He stopped his narrative and humbly waited for his master's ire to explode.

Tecúm kept silent, mulling the dilemma of this man, one of his best friends. He could not blame him for escaping, saving the rest of his party, and running to warn them. He could not condemn him for something that was beyond his power to control, like unknown weapons and beasts of attack. The news he had brought were beyond the worst news he had expected. In a soft voice he again welcomed his friend and reassured him that, given the circumstances of his predicament, he did the proper thing, saving the rest of his party and delivering the warning. He told him to go and rest, exclaiming that his services would be needed shortly. Vukub was so grateful to his friend for allowing him to save face and conserve his rank and dignity in front of his men and his commanders.

Nima and his war chief, Kakupatak, continued grilling the other soldiers, searching for answers, looking for clues that could help them neutralize the menace moving their way. Both commanders filled the gaps in the information with pertinent questions until they were satisfied that no more details could be gathered.

Once the warriors departed, Tecúm and Kakupatak continued their discussion until late in the evening. They both were raking their brains to find ways to arrest this tidal wave of soldiers that came to invade their soil, bringing with them new arms and animals that helped them in their attacks. The aggressors were better equipped than they suspected. This new development brought more bad news for their fledgling defenses. How could they prepare to counter such weapons? At the crack of dawn, the planners went home to get a few hours' rest.

Chapter 26

"What do you mean? They escaped?" Pedro de Alvarado shouted at one of the sentinels on guard during the incursion of the now-gone intruders. He continued, "One of the marauders is now dead, the other is useless, half dead. If he does not die, we will make him talk." Alvarado walked away, fuming, berating the guards for their ineptitude. Now he knew the enemy had discovered his invading army. The surprise was gone. His opponent would be ready, waiting for the attack.

After an exhaustive search was conducted, no more spies were discovered; the situation of the camp came back to near normal. After some more minor delays, the contingent started to march again. The captured spy, mercifully, had died from massive blood loss despite the misplaced efforts of the "leeches" (surgeons), who were bloodletting the patient, thus accelerating his demise.

The advance slowed when the path the column was following became too narrow for the cannons and the horses to negotiate. The riders had to dismount and lead their horses slowly, with great care. The cannons again had to be disassembled and carried piece by piece on the back of the porters.

At intervals, the foliage got denser, so much so that the soldiers had to hack the creeping vines with their swords to keep the pace going; they kept moving, advancing meter by meter and mile after difficult mile. The army sometimes barely advanced two leagues in one single day.

The water became scarce. Many times it had to be carried from far away on the back of the porters. In many of the streams they encountered, the water could not be drunk because it smelled bad, like rotten eggs. In some places, the surface of the water had a yellowish coating, thick, sickly looking, and the water was hot, almost boiling, releasing a tenuous mist.

Before nightfall, when they could still see clearly, they made camp again. More sentinels than before were posted, with dogs accompanying them on their patrols. Also, more dogs were let free to roam the perimeter of the camp. The hours dragged. The troops were unnerved by the eerie silence of the woods. The close encounter with the prowlers had spooked the men.

When the morning came, Alvarado realized the army had been following the wrong road. Was he being misled by the guides? His mood became somber, about to explode into a rage. He ordered the lead guide to be brought to him at once.

As soon as the scout was within earshot, Alvarado spat, full of fury, "*Que diablos esta pasando?* [What the hell is happening?]," the interpreter translated the question for the scared guide.

Alvarado kept going, "Are you taking us in circles, or maybe you don't know the area?" He then ordered Xicotenga, the Tlaxcala cacique, to get another guide, somebody more competent than this imbecile to whom he finally admonished, "I will not tolerate your incompetence! If this ever happens again, I swear by the mantle of the apostle Santiago I will chop you in pieces and feed you to the dogs. Do you understand me?" He finally asked the terrified guide through the translator. He dismissed the scout. Alvarado was mortified; they have lost precious time.

Shortly after the incident, the march resumed. The right road was found as if by a miracle. The landscape turned monotonous; the only view for miles were trees, followed by more trees, gigantic pines, interspersed with short brambly berry bushes. The wooded panorama was a stark contrast to his barren land of Badajóz.

He kept pushing his men, spurred by pride, determination, and avarice. All that training in the river at Badajóz and later in the sandy beaches of Cádiz was paying off. His troops were hardened by years of previous wars, but nevertheless, some men still grumbled with the effort of the pace. This was not as easy as it looked when they departed Oaxaca, full of bravado and ambition.

The long days turned into short nights, with little rest, then became days again. The monotony was maddening, the silence sometimes interrupted by the guttural growls of the big cats prowling in the vicinity, maybe watching them. The mastiffs were having a great time chasing birds, butterflies, squirrels, and many more small rodents.

When a narrow valley was reached, Alvarado called a halt. The place had a small waterfall with fresh, crystalline, and cool water that collected into a shallow pond. The bone-tired soldiers plopped to the ground. The porters relieved themselves of their burdens without asking permission from their masters. The slaves didn't care anymore.

The tired cooks got to their chores, and soon a rustic dinner was rapidly prepared. The men ate the food as if they were about to lose it to unknown forces. The food was mostly the meat of the animals hunted the previous day. Alvarado realized that the men charged with hunting were exposed to the marauders prowling the forests. They knew these woods; they moved like ghosts.

After a short meal, a lonely soldier started playing his guitar. Soon, several more men joined the music, singing their raunchy melodies, some remembering faraway lands, lost loves, ancient feuds that spoke of death and tragedy, mixed with some romance and chivalry.

"Rodrigo," Alvarado addressed his cousin Rodrigo Sosa, "supervise the posting of the guards. I don't want a repeat of what happened the other night when the sentinels were caught napping. Double the number of guards, give them some mastiffs. Unleash them, let them roam free." By now the mastiffs knew the smell of the Indians and the other men traveling with the force.

Alvarado continued, "Make sure the men posted don't fall asleep. Severe punishment will be dispensed to anyone that succumbs to sleep while they are on guard. I want you to see to it personally. Do you understand me?" He then dismissed his cousin Rodrigo.

After he was sure his orders would be carried out as he had directed, Alvarado went looking for Juan Godinez, one of the two clerics he had selected to accompany the expedition. Pedro had developed a good friendship and a newfound respect for this priest when he realized that this man indeed followed the precepts of his calling. He was honest, humble and merciful; did not drink or swear unnecessarily. Godinez was well versed in Latin and Greek. He knew the scriptures and was an avid reader, especially of poetry to which Alvarado was greatly attracted.

Back in Cádiz, where the two met, Alvarado had asked Father Godinez to complement his reading and writing. Alvarado turned to be a quick study, an eager learner, persistent to the point that soon he was able to read and write his own poems, which were always dedicated to Raquel Fuentes, that beauty he unwillingly left behind in La Esperanza when he and his brothers had to flee the town to avoid capture by the town's guard. He missed her presence terribly. Though to be honest, more recently he had been finding more and more solace in Doña Luisa's bronzed arms.

Luisa was slowly replacing the other woman with her patience, cunning, and smarts. She had become the most sought-after counselor by Pedro de Alvarado. Initially, Luisa had accepted Alvarado as her master, but more recently she had found herself more attracted to his endearments, by now eagerly participating in sexual exchanges with her master and new love. Maybe she really loved him, she thought with some despair.

The next day, Alvarado and his troops enjoyed a well-deserved rest. The horses and the mules were checked for injuries; they were groomed and properly fed. Meantime, the mastiffs kept roaming the camp, vigilant to any change in the routine, watching, their eyes full of menace, searching for intruders.

Pedro de Alvarado dispensed some time to Valor, his dog, for which the animal was so gratified that it kept growling contentedly, bouncing, pirouetting like a little child.

The soldiers took time to bathe, their filthy clothes washed and mended by the slaves. Some men even shaved and trimmed their tresses.

Doña Luisa, with an armed escort and a couple of her maids, took a brief absence to compose herself. Her monthly gift was playing havoc with her thighs. She also needed some privacy; she wanted to think about her life, her future that by now was forever hitched to Alvarado's. Was she becoming like a Spaniard woman? What did her people think of her? Was she despised as Alvarado was? She could not even talk to her father, Xicotenga, who, by all intent and purposes, was practically an "honored" prisoner of Alvarado. Even if she wanted or was able to escape, where could she go? By now all the people were aware of her relationship with Pedro de Alvarado. She would have to accommodate her feelings and loyalties. As a woman, her choices were limited in those societies, hers and the Spanish. She was not allowed to express opinions, to discuss with other men, let alone with other women. Her only consolation was that Alvarado treated her with some respect and valued her guidance.

Meanwhile, Alvarado was lost in deep thought; his mind went back to Raquel Fuentes. He still could not completely forget those alluring green eyes, that glorious auburn hair, those luscious lips that he briefly kissed only once. His mind kept wandering between Raquel and Doña Luisa.

Green eyes kept melting into dark ones. Pale, rosy skin was supplanted by a bronzed one.

He thought of his uncle Alejandro and his plucky wife, Sara. They had decided to stay in Oaxaca, tending his carpentry shop that was becoming more prosperous as the demands for new housing increased. Alejandro and Sara had "bought"—appropriated with the help of Governor Alvarado—a large property near the palace.

Sara, with her intellect and grace, had captivated the few ladies recently arrived from Spain. Sara had already planted an amazing garden. Using local flowers and trees with the help of local laborers, she had transformed it into an oasis where the birds came frequently to bathe in the fountains, lending an air of musical delight during the sunny days. He remembered them with fondness, maybe even love. His uncle had been so kind to him, who treated him like a son. Sara had been extremely gracious and understanding; she had done her best to pull him through his deepest moments of despair. She also helped him to remedy his deficiencies in reading and writing. They were such good people, unselfish and unpretentious. Alvarado, in a rare moment of religious fervor, silently asked God to bless and protect them. He even briefly prayed to the apostle Santiago to keep guarding them.

Alvarado's quest was to become rich and powerful and to one day return famous to La Esperanza and ask Raquel to be his wife, to marry him. His destiny had changed when, against his will and good intentions, he had to escape with his brothers and cousin Rodrigo, to run for his life. Now he was in this solitary place, on a road leading to God knew where. His eyes were closed, and he was half asleep.

Twack. An arrow flew by, missing his neck by scant centimeters to lodge in the trunk of the tree against which he was reclining. Certainly, his patron, the apostle Santiago, was watching and protecting him. Immediately he stood up and started to bark orders.

The alarm was raised. Everybody got on alert, looking for the ones responsible for the attack.

Silently another group of K'iche soldiers had gotten closer to their camp, masking their scent with castor oil, which, they had found, confused the dogs' keen noses. By Tojil, the oil had worked to perfection! Finally the marauders had found a way to neutralize the hounds. They had to go back to the capital and inform their lord, Tecúm, of their success. This crucial finding could not wait to be reported.

Before they disengaged, the intruders felled two more soldiers, hitting them in the head with a deadly volley of *bodoques*, the hardened clay pellets released from the *hondas*, the slingshots each warrior carried. Taking advantage of the confusion, the soldiers soon melted into the woods; again they had become ghosts, lost in a world of greenery only they knew well.

Once the alarm was over, the camp returned to near normal; the intrusion had taken the defenders by surprise. Alvarado wondered how the savages were able to get so close, inside the defense perimeter, to the point that he was almost killed by an arrow!

Pedro discussed with his men the most recent events. Questions were asked, but nobody knew the answers. A new perimeter was established, enlarged, with more sentinels and mastiffs.

An uneasy calm descended on the place. The new day faded into glorious colors in the sky, another night came, full of dread, almost everybody expecting to be struck by one of those damned clay pellets or a lost arrow that could end their lives or, worse, wound them, which amounted to a slow and painful death.

The next morning, the march was resumed. The soldiers were extremely wary, hyper-alert, afraid, all unnerved. The eerie silence of the forest nearby, mixed with the cacophony of the birds, filled their minds with an unfounded terror. This was not their usual grounds; they were used at open fields with the cavalry charging first, the footmen following close behind.

The K'iche warriors shadowing the advancing army kept their eyes peeled open, watching every movement, recording in their minds crucial details of the forces marching for their commander's information and analysis. After a few more days of watching, the leader of the group determined that this armed force was en route to attack their beloved capital, K'umarkaj. The alarm had to be raised; they had to warn their Nima Rajpop Achij, Prince Tecún, of the imminent danger coming their way.

The long trek back home began the next day, before the sun was up. The soldiers didn't march at night without torches, which could illuminate the most treacherous paths they were to follow; the information they carried was so important to be derailed by a night accident. They set a grueling pace, resting only briefly to get some water and a few morsels to eat. Maybe, they thought, the intelligence they carried could somehow change the overwhelming odds they faced. Unfortunately, the prowlers didn't get that much information on the horses and the horsemen, neither about the short russet-colored tubes. What were those?

Why did the foreigners treat them with so much care? They seemed so heavy, their poor brethren bent with the weight. They had never seen cannons; neither were they aware of the destructive power of these weapons. The intelligence gatherers were also unawares of the deadly assault the cavalry could mount. Not a single one of them had heard the loud boom the cannons could make when fired; nobody had witnessed the destruction such weapons could wreak. The K'iche was not familiar with most metals. They were still using weapons made of stone and wood. The defenders would be like babies in the woods when the Spaniards released their mighty weapons against them. They would practically be defenseless.

Why did the K'iche, despite their gigantic advances in astronomy, as far as was known, never develop the wheel? Was it because of the ruggedness of their land? Or maybe they were not practical men?

Chapter 27

"Nima Tecúm," his war chief said, "the delegation sent to the K'akchiquels and the Tz'utujils is back. They are waiting to see you. Can I show them in?"

Ahau Galel, Tecúm, responded immediately, "Bring them in. I'm anxious to find out what is the answer to my proposal."

Ixpiyacoc, one of the delegates and another soldier that accompanied him in the mission, were ushered in. Ixpiyacoc addressed his lord, Tecúm. "Nima, your offer to them to join forces with us to repel the invaders was turned down. Acajal and Xahil, their leaders, were adamant in their refusal. They even threatened that they will fight along the foreigners against us," he concluded his short, discouraging response.

An ominous hush descended on the chamber. The dignitaries receiving the news were baffled at this response and the implied threat. Nima Tecúm and his war chief could not understand why these caciques had allied themselves with the Spaniards. Was it spite? Were they trying to carry favor with the foreign devils? What was their purpose? It was true that most of the times they were at war with one another, but the most recent truce had lasted a long time. Now it was different. The invaders threatened to take their lands, to wipe out their temples, to enslave their people. How come they were so blind? They shared the same blood, the same language. Their gods were almost the same. Why then? It was madness!

After a few minutes of reflection, Nima Tecúm spoke, "Very well, we are alone to face this enemy. Our brethren at Zaculeu are too far away to lend us a hand in this conflict, We will have to fight this invading force by ourselves, try to do our best to repel them." With a heavy heart he sat down, his chest filled with a dark premonition of the horrors to come. Their very survival was at stake. He knew that when the war came, it would be to the end.

The discussion continued. A decision was made to send the children, women, and the elders to the neighboring kingdom of Zaculeu, seat of the kingdom populated by the Mam people, distant cousins to the K'iche whose cacique had always been friendly to their people. The kingdom was situated away in the mountains to the north, several days' march. Tecún knew their cacique would welcome and keep his people safe. Nevertheless, Tecún would send a special envoy to request asylum and protection for his soon-to-depart kindred. To that purpose, Tecún dictated an official petition. The messenger left the same day. Time was getting shorter.

When the information collected by the party sent to assess the Spaniard troops was analyzed, another weapon against the mastiffs had being found. By pure chance, it was discovered that the sound of the *pitos*, a whistle made of clay, was so loud and bothersome to the dogs' sensitive ears, acute enough to send them whimpering, cowing, disoriented, refusing to obey the orders of their handlers despite threats to that effect. Tecúm ordered that the *pitos* be carried by the troops to be used when their attack commenced.

During the recon mission, another crucial piece of intelligence had been obtained. The scouts observed that at one point, the men riding the *caballos* came down from the back of the animal, the rider going his own separate way, the horse taken away to be fed and taken care of. At first, even when they seemed to be one body when they were together, moving like a single piece, this was not the case. The beast, as opposed to the K'iche belief, was not the *nahual*, the protector of the rider. They were not one unit! A plan was hatched. By using longer *lanzas*, the K'iche warrior would be able to first slaughter the animal and then kill the horseman.

Nima Rajpop Achij, Tecúm, ordered to equip as many men as possible with these longer spears. The planners, unfortunately, forgot or didn't know that the Spaniards wore a breastplate made of a material they were not familiar with, making it more difficult to slay the rider. They also wielded a large metallic pike that gave the user a longer reach.

The most fearsome weapon of the aggressor was the long stick that with a loud boom belched fire. What could they do against such deadly thunder? All the planners agreed that probably the best defense would be to stay as far away from the boom as was possible. It was also decided to reinforce the cotton cuirass the K'iche officers used with several layers of bark embedded in the cotton. Later on, during the initial stages of the battle, to their detriment, the K'iche would learn that most of the measures adopted would be insufficient to neutralize the devastating firepower and the most advanced military tactics of the Spaniards. They would almost be defenseless.

The odds were overwhelming; the K'iche nation was doomed from the beginning! But they could not just surrender; their whole civilization was imperiled. Hundreds of years of learning were in danger to be wiped out. What else could they do?

The K'iche people were, most of the times, a peaceful one, but now they were being attacked without a motive, except the thirst for bounty and expansionism of the foreigners. The invaders have been adamant and relentless when they presented to the Nima Rajpop Achij, Tecúm their lopsided peace offer. The menace was more ominous because of the alliance of their sworn enemies, the K'akchiquels and the Tz'utujils, who, in a last act of treachery, had threatened to fight alongside the white people. As far as Tecún could remember he had done nothing to provoke the invasion. He could not believe that the time he kept the emissaries of Alvarado waiting was a reason enough to invade. But was it possible? He asked himself.

Chapter 28

"Cristobal," Alvarado called Captain Cristobal Olid. "I have decided to pay a visit to the cacique of the Cachiquels, Acajal and then stop by to see Xahil, the cacique of the Tz'utujils. I need to enlist their help in the coming fight against those heathens up north, the despicable Quichés," he spat with disdain and venom. "You will leave early next morning and let them know of my command." Alvarado continued speaking, "Remind them of the promise they made to me that their warriors will join us in any future attacks against their eternal enemies. Take some twenty men and as many Indians as you want. Remember to be careful with ambushes, those barbarians are becoming bolder. Tell the caciques that I expect them with their best forces to meet with my troops close to the city we are bound for so I can instruct them on the role they will play." Alvarado dismissed Olid, his mind already dealing with the next phase of his plan, the annihilation of his unwilling enemies, the K'iche.

The next day, bright and early, the main body of the army left bound for K'umarkaj. The small contingent commanded by Cristobal Olid went another route in search of the two chieftains, Acajal and Xahil. Olid was mulling the orders his captain had given him. The instructions had been precise and didn't leave any doubt as to the purpose of them.

The march of the main attack force continued for days; no new harassments occurred. The soldiers settled in an uneasy routine; bitching at the indian slaves, catcalling among themselves, caring for the horses and mules, pampering the mastiffs, constantly complaining of the terrain. Many of them had never seen so many trees, which in some places were so close together, making the advance almost impossible, but somehow Alvarado kept pushing his men without mercy, like a man possessed, in search of his prize.

The column kept ascending the mountain, imposing peaks, some damp with the night's dew. The view was majestic, more so as they ascended more and more. The pines were gigantic in some spots, and the fragrance they emanated was soothing and hypnotizing. It was so green, with a sky a vivid blue, clear, like the cerulean color of the eyes of some of the girls they remembered from back home. Some men sighed with longing. They were so far away from their *lares* (domains).

At night, sitting by the fires, the men listened to sad songs that spoke of their native lands, accompanied by an out-of-tune guitar plucked with gusto by a soldier. There was nothing else to do. Most men were wondering when they would find the fabled metropolis, when they would meet the enemy, which by now, in their minds, had become an army composed of six-foot men with powerful muscles and bronzed skin, men that could tear them apart with their bare hands and eat them piece by piece. Many were afraid of the tales of the human sacrifices mistakenly attributed to the Maya, a nation that had never offered humans to their gods. These rituals belonged mostly to other cultures.

Once all the chores of setting the camp for the night were concluded, the soldiers went to sleep, enveloped in a ghastly silence only broken by the loud snoring and farting of the troops. Nearby, lurking in the shadows were few K'iche waiting for the soldiers to fall asleep completely. The light of the moon gave them a clear view of the encampment. They were eager to avenge the slaying of their friends a few days before.

Again, the prowlers had smeared themselves with castor oil (ricin), which they previously had found was effective in masking their scent. The intruders got closer, advancing with stealth until their leader considered they were within range for the *hondas* to be effective. The sentinels on guard were felled with direct hits to the soft spot in their heads with a deadly volley of *bodoques*, which landed silently, killing them instantaneously. Two more soldiers were killed by arrows that pierced their necks with precision. Other soldiers were lucky because they had not removed their breastplates, thus protecting them from the projectiles hurled by the attackers.

Silently as they had come, the marauders melted into the darkness and the embrace of the nearby forest. They had employed the silent tactics copied from the Spaniards, who had paid with their lives their poor vigilance.

When the change of the guard came, the bodies were discovered. The alarm was raised, but the assailants were already gone, but they had stayed close enough to be a danger, just biding their time to attack again. The K'iche soldiers were patient, silent, as if they were stalking deer. No more attacks were made; the raiding party was close, just waiting a more propitious time to again harass the invading soldiers. It had become a cat-and-mouse game, all parties involved in a deadly contest of survival.

When Alvarado woke up, he was beside himself, furious, indignantly bellowing threats and epithets. "Those bastards killed my soldiers, I will make them pay this outrage with their lives, I will fry them alive." He kept going full blast. "Were the guards sleeping?" he asked no one in particular. "They are such a bunch of incompetents! They should consider themselves lucky to be dead because, otherwise, I would have killed them with my own hands." Pedro de Alvarado kept ranting. He could not believe that veteran soldiers were taken by surprise by these savages.

What a mess, it was a disgrace. He thought to himself that he would have to reassess the opinion he had of the Quichés. He had not prepared for guerilla warfare. Alvarado had underestimated the cunning of the Indians. He vowed that he would correct his mistakes to avoid more casualties among his soldiers.

The brightness of the moon kept the soldiers awake. The men could not go back to sleep. They kept discussing their close call. Some of them silently thanked God for sparing their lives, for their deliverance, wondering how lucky they were that somebody else had died in their place.

As soon as the sun was up, the deceased were buried in shallow graves. A short mass in their memory was said by the priests accompanying the army. The clerics entrusted their immortal souls to Jesus Christ, reminding all the living of the torments of hell awaiting them. As if this place was not hellish enough, some men complained bitterly. The soldiers grumbled loudly that they didn't even have a drop of wine to properly say good-bye to their comrades and friends.

What a disgrace, not even a little sip to make this miserable life more bearable. As good soldiers, they missed their wine. They could not even enjoy the company of a slave because the few women traveling with the army were declared out of bounds by Doña Luisa, a decision that was enforced by Alvarado and his brothers traveling with him.

Awareness was renewed; changes were made. More soldiers were detailed for guard duty. Tonight there would be no singing; no loud talk would be permitted. Many soldiers grumbled that they were being treated like children. Reluctantly they would obey; otherwise, they could pay with their lives.

Alvarado was getting worried because the advance was being delayed. He had not counted with the difficulties of the terrain, or with the constant harassment at the hands of the K'iche warriors. He was baffled, thinking where he had failed.

The information he acquired from the area before the expedition departed was at best sketchy The woods had turned to be denser than he was led to believe, the paths narrower, which made the maneuvering of the cannons especially difficult. In some stretches, the road was barely a strip of dirt flanked by gigantic trees. The weather was pleasant, but the atmosphere was spooky, creepy; the men were unnerved by the profound silence. Alvarado was told that the city they were advancing toward was a big metropolis, imposing, with many large temples and palaces full of treasures. The city at one time had a population of up to one hundred thousand people. His informers failed or didn't know about the deep ravines surrounding the citadel. The simple truth was that not even a single one of the informers had ever been to the city, let alone visited the temples. All the details provided were secondhand, greatly exaggerated, passed from person to person, family to family, with each one adding their own take on the place, like a fable.

Wisely, Alvarado decided to wait until he had better intelligence about this place, then he would choose the best way to attack. He was conscious that he had no big war machines, like trebuchets or giant ballistae. He only had four small cannons; his comfort was that as far as he knew, the K'iche had none. He consoled himself with the thought that his enemy didn't have horses or attack dogs that could make his plan of attack more complicated.

He ordered a rest of a couple of days to replenish provisions and allow the forces of the two allied caciques enough time to rendezvous with his forces. Alvarado was wondering if Olid was able to reach the two chieftains and inform them of his command.

The news was received with joy and shouts of delight by the soldiers, who were exhausted with the toll of the march, the constant harassment by the infidels. The porters were even more elated. Maybe now they could try to escape to the inviting wooded areas. The death of the few soldiers killed by the K'iche intruders had renewed their hopes of redemption. Maybe the K'iche would deliver them from the clutches of the Spaniards, though there was always the possibility that they would end up only changing masters. Would the K'iche be worse masters than the Spaniards? some wondered and delayed their decision to escape. After all, what was the point of trying to escape? They didn't know if they would be welcome by the people they were advancing against.

Alvarado summoned to his presence Pedro Portocarrero, one of his most trusted captains who had been to the city. Since he was a soldier, maybe he could give him more detailed information. Alvarado was desperate and had decided to question his captain again even when he had already done that back in Oaxaca. He respected the advice of Portocarrero. He knew that Pedro was one of the few Spanish nobles that had joined his present expedition.

Alvarado and Portocarrero had met in Cádiz during the time they were waiting for the armada to sail. Their bond was strengthened when they fought shoulder to shoulder during the *Noche Triste* in Tenochtitlán, though, somehow, Alvarado still resented the action of Portocarrero when he had refused Cortés' orders to attack, almost costing them their lives during that infamous night. Fortunately, Portocarrero had relented and finally came to their rescue, helping Alvarado and Cortés escape a certain death. More lately, Portocarrero had become indispensable to Alvarado, and he was relying on his judgment more and more. Besides, Portocarrero was a good artillery man, and his skill would be soon put to the test during the initial phase of the attack against the citadel.

Portocarrero was the first to speak. "Governor, the city is, as you already know, called Gumaarkaj or K'umarkaj. During the short time I spent there, I counted four large temples and could see from the streets few palaces. The city is surrounded by deep *barrancos* [ravines], almost impossible to negotiate. The horses would not be able to maneuver there. The main road we traversed leads to a valley with a few low mounds. A river crosses the plateau; I think they call it Olintepeque. I could not assess if the river is deep or shallow because all the time we spent there we were under guard and confined to our lodgings. I could not see any bridges. If the enemy decides to fight in the city, we will have a really difficult time. The place, from the strategic point of view, is worse than Tenochtitlán. I believe our best option will be to lure the Quiché to fight us in the open, in the valley, where you can use the horses, the mastiffs, and the cannons to your advantage. Also, in the flat terrain, the footmen can maneuver with more ease."

Alvarado kept mulling his dilemma, questioning Portocarrero incessantly, probing and getting the most of the little intelligence his captain had been able to gather from his brief stay in the city of Gumaarkaj.

After Alvarado dismissed Portocarrero, he went in search of Doña Luisa. He craved her company, her advice. He liked to hear her melodious voice. He was becoming more and more dependent on her judgment. She had proven to be extremely smart, with a special knack for little details. Her words were becoming a sore need for him. Maybe he was falling for her. Raquel was still a powerful memory, but day by day, more distant, ethereal, less alluring. Was this land changing him? It was so bountiful, so green, so vast. He had never seen in his short life so many animals, so many large predators and beautiful birds. He had been particularly taken with a small bird with deep crimson chest and a long curved tail the natives called quetzal.

Xicotenga, Doña Luisa's father, had told him that this bird was revered by the K'iche as a symbol of freedom and could not live in captivity. He had further added that Prince Ahau Galel-Tecún was protected by this avian creature that sometimes during war, this warrior could fly to the skies and from up high could strike his enemies with bolts of fire taken from the sun. At that time, Alvarado did not pay that much attention, thinking that maybe it was a myth. Or could it be like the apostle Santiago his own guardian who protected him? Alvarado thought this possible, especially after his close call with an arrow a few days back. He would have to question Luisa about this legend.

Alvarado noticed that the nights were becoming less cold, the trees more sparse. Maybe they were getting closer to the valley.

They had been on the march for almost three months. Was it already the month of April? he wondered. He fell asleep thinking of his mother, whom he had not seen since they left Badajóz, where they had come looking to have a good time in La Esperanza but ended up in this new continent. Was she still alive? Did she receive the last money they sent her before sailing? Several years had gone by. He briefly thought with resentment of that irascible priest that belted him without mercy. He did not think about his father at all! Most of his family was traveling with him, his brothers, Hernando, Gómez, Jorge, as well as his cousin Rodrigo.

He thought that his native land didn't have any large incentive that would make him wish to return to it. He was, after all, the son of a man that no longer had any big standing in the community, let alone the kingdom of Spain. He was as poor as the most indigent of his soldiers, but here, in Oaxaca, he was the governor, the ruler chosen by his mentor, Cortés, to advance the designs of the crown. He had to succeed. There was no room for failure. He could not return to his country empty-handed and in disgrace. No way! He would do the impossible to prevail. His dreams were full of large riches, beautiful clothes, and the adulation of the members of the court of his king, Carlos V.

His mind kept drifting to the time he and his brothers spent with those bawdy gypsies. He wondered if they safely reached their destination of Compostela. He fondly recollected the spicy food they were offered, the warm friendship of the lovely women, their openness. He was really envious that those girls could read and write. Why were those people so despised by the Catholics? What was their crime? They were no different than the Catholics, except for their bright and gaudy garments and their tendency to "borrow" things from their neighbors. Where were they now? The memory of Sarita was still fresh in his memory. How was she able to divine his future? To tell him that he would have two loves? How did she know that he would meet and possess Luisa? Was she in league with Lucifer? He shortly dismissed such thoughts. They were good people!

Chapter 29

"Do I really have to wear those feathers around my ankles and wrists?" Nima Tecúm asked his armorer-valet. The *armorer* fitting him answered, "Yes, Nima. It is our tradition for the Nima Rajpop Achij to wear the symbols of his *nahual*, in your case, our sacred quetzal." He added, "After all, there are only but a few feathers you have to wear. Remember, they will give you protection against the enemy; they will make you as nimble as the quetzal, your guardian angel, your protector. They would make you fly above these mere mortals, close to the sun, and from the heights you will smite your adversaries." The *armorer* concluded with the greatest conviction.

Tecún was somewhat mollified, but after some thought, he agreed to wear the symbols. Tecúm would also be fitted with a short off-white tunic embroidered with multiple bees, the sign of prosperity for the Maya. His powerful chest would be bare, with no jewelry. His headdress would be a magnificent *penacho* made of lustrous feathers of exotic birds trapped especially for his investiture as supreme commander. Finally, his feet would be encased in sandals of the finest leather, pummeled until they were as soft as linen; the soles were sturdy and thick.

His official inauguration was fast approaching. The *armorer* kept fussing some more until he was satisfied his lord would look regal as befitting his rank and lineage. He would be the supreme commander of the K'iche nation, the last Maya people left to oppose the tidal wave of invaders arriving from far away. No other groups would be coming to support them.

By now, Nima Tecúm had learned that these new invaders hiked from a faraway land called Spain, that they spoke a strange language called Castilian. His informers, escapees from the clutches of the Spaniards, had told him that they were, with few exceptions, cruel, gross, boisterous, illiterate, greedy, that they worshipped a God called Jesus Christ and that the two priests with them were pious men. Tecún had also found that these soldiers carried a long knife, deadly in their hands, they called *espada*. The soldiers also used a short, thin, extremely sharp knife named *daga-dagger*. Their breast was encased in a shiny, thick, heavy metal piece that protected the user from lances and swords called *coraza* (breastplate). Their head was covered by a heavy metal hat-like the men referred to as *casco* (helmet). Over their shins, some soldiers sported greaves, a hard metal contraption that protected their legs.

After leaving the armorer's premises, Tecún set out for his headquarters, where Kakupatak, the war chief, was waiting for him. On entering his quarters, Tecún was happily surprised to see Yum Kaax Ik, the Lord Chancellor. Yum Kaax had been a friend of his family for generations, and Tecúm felt a certain fondness for the craggy man. He paid a lot of attention to his advice, which so far had been accurate. This time, though, Yum had no better or any news to impart and kept somewhat silent, waiting in the wings to see if his lord, Tecún, had any new commands for him.

Kakupatak succinctly gave his report about the failed mission to the K'akchiquels and the Tz'utujils. He informed Nima Tecúm that they were adamant in their refusal to join forces with them, instead boasting that by now they were allied with the invading Spaniards. Kakupatak further added that no argument could sway them to change their minds; they firmly believed that the Spaniards were their new protectors and benefactors. The K'iche nation was left alone, abandoned to their fate. They would have to face the enormous wave marching relentlessly toward their borders. Would they find a way to stop the menace?

"We are alone," Nima Tecúm stated, full of despair. He had hoped that their neighbors would see reason and come to their side, but no, they would not help them. Tecún was now convinced. He continued, "Our forces will have to fight alone against those overwhelming forces. I hope we can prevail."

The strategic session continued nonstop for few more hours. More plans were made, revised, adopted, or discarded as impractical. Some new ideas were introduced, discussed once; then again until they were satisfied nothing else could be put to good use.

The K'iche nation was now in a war footing, isolated, betrayed by their ancient enemies, the K'akchiquels and the Tz'utujils. Tecúm's spies had warned him that the enemy forces were on the march to join the Spaniards.

Tecúm ordered his scouts to keep track of their movements and alert him if they got too close to the city.

Because of the war looming so close, his installation as Nima Rajpop Achij was a subdued affair, still solemn, but with less pomp and circumstance. People were busy tending to the demands of the imminent war. Present at the ceremony were members of the four royal families of the kingdom, with Ixchel slightly in the background but still in a prominent and visible place as his future queen. Her mother, Ixmucané, and her sister, K'etzalin, were also in attendance, as well as Kakupatak, his mentor and friend. Yum Kaax Ik, as Lord Chancellor, swore him in.

Absent were the music of the marimbas and the haunting notes of the *chirimillas*. The only sounds were the monotonous beat of the *tuns*. They sounded as if they were announcing an impending disaster, as if their beat prophesied a great wave of pain, suffering, and death instead of celebrating the elevation of their favorite son to the most prominent post in the kingdom.

The citizenry were sad and subdued because they loved Ahau Galel, Tecún Umán, their Nima Rajpop Achij, but could not celebrate given the grave state of war. No *chicha* was permitted as was customary during historic celebrations.

Every waking hour of Tecún was consumed with demands for this or that detail, visits to the garrisons, supervision of defenses, training of the new recruits that by now swelled the number of troops close to 8,400, many new to the war effort, with almost no prior training. They were mostly farmers, uprooted from their agricultural labors, called to help in the defense of their country. All of them were honored to have been called to serve, willing to sacrifice their lives in defense of their homeland, their values, beliefs, and traditions.

Apocalyptic events were about to be unleashed on their nation; a culture of the most sophisticated people of all history were close to being wiped off from the face of the earth by ignorant hordes, spurred by greed, obscure beliefs, and a thirst for destruction. A hushed, ominous silence had taken over the once bustling city. The citizens walked silently, as if they were afraid their voices could be heard by the enemy. Their heads were bowed, trying not to offend the god wind, afraid it could push the invaders even closer to their beloved city. All were silently praying for a miracle, something that could save their great city from the unknown enemy, a foe they had never seen before.

Despite their fears, most citizens were determined to sell their lives at a heavy price. They vowed to be brave and face the attack with all their might. They all trusted their captain general, Ahau Galel, Tecúm. Many fighters were detailed to the task of sheltering and saving large amounts of corn and beans in case the city became under siege. Water was no problem since they still had easy access to the river. The elders were guiding the young ones, telling them to be brave, that Tojil, their god, would protect them and that Q'uq'matz, the white-feathered serpent, guardian of their kingdom—would be with them, fighting to repel the invaders.

In the temples, a thin cloud of smoke could be seen escaping the premises. The priests were eagerly burning copal incense to assuage the ire of the gods, asking clemency for their transgressions that were none, other than being in the way of the greedy foreigners.

Women, under the direction of Ixmucané and her daughters, Princesses Ixchel and K'etzalin, were busy tending to the needs of old and young people, getting ready for the impending exodus to the city of Zaculeu, as was planned before by Tecún and Kakupatak. All were infected with the prospect of impending doom. The women were worried about their husbands, sons, that they knew would inevitably perish in the war.

While the women worked they kept praying silently, suppressing tears of rage and impotence asking to themselves why men were so cruel, why they were so blind and bent on destruction. Their gentle souls could not comprehend the dark forces behind the motives of the Spaniards. They were so alien, so different to any people they had seen before. They asked themselves why some of the soldiers covered their faces with hair and why some of the few they saw before were so pale, with eyes devoid of color and warmth.

Chapter 30

Walking the valley, Nima Tecúm and Kakupatak, the war chief, were discussing the best options for setting the defenses. Both commanders and their entourage were following the margins of the Olintepeque River, whose waters flowed meandering across the basin, like a giant serpent, with a slightly east-to-west direction. The stream was placid, about two-hundred feet wide at its widest margin and narrowed in some spots to around one hundred feet.

By now both commanders were aware of the fast way the horses could move and agreed that probably the best way to hinder the free movements of these animals would be to dig *zanjas* (trenches) in front and beyond the margins of the river, parallel to it, in the shallowest sections of the current. The *zanjas* would be excavated to a depth of six feet and twelve feet wide with the hope that this might curtail the advance of the horses and the mastiffs. Two sets of trenches would be excavated—one immediately before the river, with about two hundred feet of dead space until the margins of the water, the other set of trenches across the river, with no dead space before it. Whoever would cross the no-man's-land would be faced with a pile of dirt, the result from the dug out earth would be piled in front of trenches to form walls, like ramparts, from which heights the archers and the soldiers with *hondas* could discharge their deadly missiles. In the second parapet, at convenient intervals, narrow gates would be placed to allow the warriors to move to this second bastion in case the first line of defense was overrun by the advancing forces. The defenders were counting that the depth of the river in the other areas would impede the advance of the aggressors and give the defenders some sorely needed advantage. Fortunately, most of the K'iche warriors were good swimmers and wore light or no armor at all that could encumber their retreat, should they be forced to jump to the waters.

The *zanjas* would be excavated by *zappers* (farmers), many coming from faraway places from which they had been summoned by their masters. Tecúm and Kakupatak were earnestly awaiting their arrival, which hopefully would happen in the next few days.

"Kakupatak," Tecúm said to his war chief, "I worry that the river may impede our retreat if our two line of defense are breached, then we would have to move to the streets of the city that is not easily defended. Do you think we should store some materiel at strategic points?" He proceeded, "Those brutes they call *perros* give me grief. They look vicious and powerful. They are so silent that is unnerving, though Ixpiyacoc and Vukub noticed that the sounds of the *pitos* sent the beasts whimpering, disoriented, and they could not be persuaded to attack despite threats from their handlers. Order the soldiers to carry them. We will use them in battle when the animals are released. Maybe, just maybe, this can somehow help."

In the last few days, the hunters had been busy getting as many animals as they could bring in to feed the troops in case of a prolonged siege. Fortunately, corn and fruits were in abundance. The question both chieftains asked themselves was for how long they could survive.

Nima Tecúm and Kakupatak had previously agreed that women, children, and nonessential men would be sent away to Zaculeu, the capital of the Mam Empire, in a few days' time. The Mam shared almost the same ancestry with the Maya-K'iche, though they were not as pure as them. The relationships with the Mam nation were cordial. Tecúm had already received reassurances that their cacique would welcome his people with open arms. The dilemma for Nima Tecúm in sending their people to this place was that the Mam would be the next target should the K'iche fail to defeat the Spaniard. Then the Mam would be squeezed between the Spaniards up north that would be coming from Oaxaca and the forces already here. The tidal wave was getting stronger, almost inevitable, a great river of sorrow that threatened to destroy anything in its path. Tecúm was sure this group was only the tip of the spear that would pierce his nation, appropriate their lands, and enslave them. He wondered where they did go wrong.

Were the gods unhappy with them? His mind kept playing with new, discouraging scenarios, desperately trying to find a way to repel the aggressors, to make them vanish. It was becoming a nightmare. He kept walking the field of operations, canvassing the defenses, trying to pinpoint the ideal spots to position his troops. He thought with sadness that so many of them were so young, so inexperienced. The time left to properly prepare them was so short. What a monumental quandary! He needed a miracle, and he fervently prayed for one.

Finally, when the sun was fast disappearing behind the majestic mountains in the horizon, Nima Tecúm decided to head home. He would visit Ixchel. It had been a few days since he last visited his betrothed. By Cacoch—god creator, how he missed her sweet voice, her lovely eyes, the silkiness of her hair. He was afraid that he might lose her forever, but he quickly dismissed those dark thoughts. He had to stay positive, upbeat. He could not allow doubts to take possession of his mind.

When Ahau Galel reached her palace, he was immediately shown in, with even more courtesy than before he was elected Nima Rajpop Achij. The steward of the house now saw him as the supreme commander of his people, as the prospective new lord of the house. Besides, he truly loved and respected his lord, Ahau, Tecún.

When Ixchel came in, he could not help but rush to hold her in his arms, to give her a bear hug. For her part, Ixchel, also on instinct, returned his embrace, melding her body with his, all conventional norms forgotten for the time being, relegated to the urgent need to communicate with him. A sense of urgency had gripped both, pushing them to be bold, to taste the sweetness of the loved person, to get strength from the warmth of the other. In silence they continued holding each other, happy, fulfilled to be so close. Tecúm caressed her silky hair, kissed her temples, nibbled her earlobes, and soon was kissing her sweet mouth, tasting those luscious lips with a passion he didn't know he possessed. Her breath mingled with his, coming in short gasps, at times more frenetic. She caressed his naked back, felt his powerful muscles respond to her touch, to demand more and more. Finally, with a supreme, concerted effort, they separated, content that finally they had found and barely explored the pleasure the close contact brought to their bodies.

They had not expected that it would be so powerful, exhilarating and conducive to such deep fulfillment. The physical force had become so powerful, well beyond their human endurance. They wanted so bad to discover their newfound closeness, but reluctantly they pulled apart one from each other, slightly ashamed of having been so bold and succumb to the attraction.

Once Ahau recovered his composure, he exclaimed, "Ixchel, I miss you. I feel like dying every time I have to go. Honestly, I wish we were common peasants that could elope and run to the mountains, but we are encumbered with our responsibilities. People look to us for example." He got quiet and pensive, waiting for her reaction.

"Ahau, you know how much my heart aches for you, I would also gladly run away with you, far away from this terrifying fate awaiting our nation. I'm really afraid." She proceeded, "Ahau, I have the premonition, a feeling that I will never see you again, that my life will end soon. Please, tell me that I'm wrong. I have discussed with my mother and my sister our impending escape. There are so many children and elders to save. I pray to Jacawitz to give me courage, to grant me wisdom to carry this task to completion. I wish you were coming with us, but you are needed here to lead our men into battle. Please, promise me that you would be careful, I won't be able to live without you." She was barely able to control her emotions, holding her tears. She didn't want Ahau to see her whimpering; she had to be strong for him.

Their intimate conversation continued until they were interrupted by her mother, Ixmucané, when she summoned them to dinner. The meal again was incomparable and extremely tasty. Was this perception augmented by their recent experience? Ahau wondered. But they were not too eager to eat. They had partially satiated their needs with their close encounter. They were cognizant that soon she would depart on her mission of mercy and survival, all alone, frightened, threading the *cerros*, trying to escape capture and with it certain servitude. She trembled with this thought.

His heart was rebelling against such injustice, against their predicament. But he had to be strong; he had to help her to carry her task. They both silently agreed that there was no other option if they wanted their culture to survive. Then they promised to themselves to carry on their mission with dignity and courage. They were of the Maya people. They were nobility. They also knew that they had no other alternative.

Chapter 31

ext morning, Nima Tecúm continued his inspection of the troops. A flood of pride filled his heart. The recruits were young, but their eyes shone with eagerness, everyone raving to prove themselves worthy of the trust their commander had bestowed on them.

The time the women and children would depart was fast approaching. Tecúm got busy with many tasks, thinking about the time when his beloved Ixchel would head for the mountains, but his mind soon became engrossed in the minutiae of the preparations for the battle to come. His pace was slow but determined. He didn't want to miss any small detail that could lead to defeat.

The night was about to descend. The exiles would be led by his fiancée Ixchel, supported by her mother, Ixmucané, and her sister, K'etzalin. They had been working feverishly, making the necessary preparations for the long trek. Few nonessential men, mostly elderly, were to accompany the group. The date of departure had been set for tomorrow night when the moon would be hidden by clouds as forecasted by the astronomers. The whole city was energized by the monumental enterprise.

Inexorably, the night of departure was approaching. Tecúm was sitting facing Ixchel, giving her last-minute instructions, making sure all the details of the coming action were completely covered, that she had understood his explanations.

He was trying to protect her and his people from any unforeseen danger. Tecúm had drilled Ixchel with the many details of the secret path the fugitives would follow in their escape. He made her aware of the many places in the *cerros* where they could hide, the many streams that could provide them with freshwater. The party would be carrying dried meat, dried fruits, and *ticucos* that the K'iche carried in long treks.

"Ixchel, my love," Ahau said, "my heart and my prayers will go with you. You have no idea how hard it is for me to let you go, to see you unwillingly walk away from my life. I thank you for your patience and understanding during my long absences. Your love and devotion has sustained me during those long nights and days of uncertainty. Your love has given me so much courage, that much-needed lift to my spirit. Our way of life is at risk. I promise you I will defend it with valor and honor, with my life if necessary." He kept going, "May Cacoch our god creator, guide and protect you and your family. I promise to look for you as soon as it is safe and the invaders have been defeated. I would personally come to Zaculeu to bring you and your family back to our capital."

"Ahau, life of my eyes, light of my days, you give me honor to think of me in these demanding times. I love you with all my heart and I wish I could stay by your side to face any danger coming our way, but I know we need to think about the children and the elders. Our children represent the hope to preserve our lineage and our traditions alive. The elders anchor us to our past, to our gods and *nahuals*." She took a brief respite and continued, "Your love makes me so happy, I could not ask for more."

In another rare moment of boldness, she embraced him, and she kissed Ahau in the mouth with such passion and longing that he was surprised at this display of open love in such a reserved and traditional woman. She was so afraid for his safety; she wondered if she would ever see him again alive, but she kept a straight face, holding her tears, until finally she was able to say good-bye to the man of her dreams, the fountain of her happiness. She knew that on the night of departure, it would be hard to be alone with him. This was the last time they would see each other, no more opportunities for embracing and saying good-bye.

Tecúm, summoning his inner strength, embraced Ixchel a final time, searing forever in his mind the outlines of that precious face, the womanly scent of her body, then went in search of her mother and sister to bid them farewell and give some more final instructions. He embraced them and with a heavy heart and with great dignity departed. He was about to face his destiny.

After Ahau left, Ixpiyacoc, his friend, came looking for K'etzalin. He finally had found the courage to tell her about his feelings. When he saw his beloved girl, Ixpiyacoc advanced toward her, took her hands in his, and declared, "K'etzalin, now I know that I have loved you all my life, since we were children, but I was afraid that you would turn me down. I want you to know that when this war is over, I intend to ask your mother and Ahau, your father-to-be, for your hand. I hope you will grant me the honor to say yes. I cannot conceive any other way." He was full of hope, waiting.

K'etzalin responded, "Ixpiyacoc, sweetie, silly sweetie, you have been on my mind forever. Many times I felt so frustrated because you didn't tell me about your feelings. I'm so happy to finally know I was not mistaken in thinking that you also love me." She then took his hands and came closer to him, wishing to kiss his forehead, his lips and his neck. But this wouldn't be proper; they were not yet engaged. What would he think of her? Would he be ashamed? She was frustrated, but happy. The soft perfume of K'etzalin and her closeness was driving Ixpiyacoc wild with desire, but he refrained from making a blunder. He didn't want to lose this lovely woman. He made a mental promise that he would come back to marry her.

The newfound lovers spent a long time talking about their dreams until the time came for him to depart. Duty was calling, insistent, relentless.

Nearby, in the shadows, her mother, Ixmucané, silently thanked Jacawitz, the god creator, for finally allowing her daughter a brief moment of happiness. Her heart told her that they would never see each other again, at least not on this earth. She cried silently. It was not fair! Ixmucané thought bitterly why life was so cruel. How was it that some people only found love in the bleakest hour of their lives? But at least she saw her happy. But she was not ungrateful. The gods had been merciful with her and her two lovely girls, who finally had found the men of their dreams. She promised herself to do the impossible to keep them safe.

Ixmucané still could remember the last time she had visited the kingdom of the Mam in happier times with her husband, many of their friends, and servants. They were mere memories now. She sighed contentedly. Ixmucané could still picture the way they were greeted by the cacique and his entourage. Ah, those were happier times, full of promise for the future. But now, the white invaders had desecrated her land in search of riches. Even when she had not met them before, she knew that she hated them with all her heart. She fervently prayed that Tecún, her future son-in-law would be victorious against the aggressors. She willed him to pummel the invaders, to make them regret having come to their lands. She was so full of hope. Fervently, Ixmucané continued praying to her gods, asking for a miracle, requesting deliverance.

Chapter 32

The following night, unseen by the spies sent by Alvarado, under cover of darkness, the women, children, and elders left the city bound for Zaculeu, miles away in the mountains. The road they would be traveling was hidden in the bushes, known only to them. It would bring the fugitives directly to their destination, with any luck avoiding any scouts sent by the invaders.

The feet of the adults were covered by soft *caites* (sandals) to mask their footsteps. A few hours before, the children were given a concoction of honey and sarsaparilla, a sedative, to prevent them from crying on leaving their parents and their homes.

Each child was carried *atuto*, on the backs of the adults. The soldiers left behind watched the exodus with a heavy lump in their throats, not knowing if they would ever see their loved ones again. A great pain gripped every heart; tears came furtively to the eyes of hardened men, who were silently praying to their gods to protect and guard their loved ones. They had said their farewells before, unseen. Soon, the muted shuffling of footsteps was lost in the darkness of the night, carrying them toward an unknown fate.

Early the next morning, even before the sun was completely up, the contingent of *zappers*, who arrived the previous night, were put to work. Their job would be to excavate the *zanjas* along the margins of the river as planned, deep enough to hinder the free displacement of the horses, denying in this way one of the advantages the Spaniards had.

Tecúm and Kakupatak had decided to dig the trenches in an overlapping way, as they had discussed many times before. They knew that with the sun, the clay excavated would become hardened, would provide the men with *hondas* an unlimited supply of clay pellets. Once the dirt was piled, it would become like a solid wall that would protect the troops, atop which the men could hurl their weapons. When the time came, the foot soldiers would leave the emplacements and engage in hand-to-hand combat with the enemy, clubbing them to death with obsidian-studded maces or impaling them with the long lances provided. At least that was the plan. No one thought of using flaming arrows. The K'iche had never faced this cunning enemy, nor didn't they know their way to conduct war. They were not aware of the cannons.

Nima Rajpop Achij, Tecúm, together with his war chief, Kakupatak, kept walking the perimeter, inspecting the preparations, probing for weak spots, encouraging the men, prodding the ones wavering, praising them for their courage. A kind word uttered here, a pat on the back dispensed there. All the soldiers were proud to see their commander walking among them, acknowledging his presence with silent bows. Many men had never seen him before; they only knew him by reputation. They knew that he belonged to the house of Tekún, and that was enough for them. He was a noble man. He was loved by the populace, who considered him one of them even when he was their cacique, the supreme commander.

The city, without the children, was silent, like a tomb, empty, devoid of life. No laughter, no scuffles, no babies crying, no mothers calling for their children to come back home. The only sounds heard were the whimpering of the small dogs left behind by their owners, mixed with the cackling of a few chickens and the ever-present crows, which sat silently atop the buildings, like bunts announcing a funeral. Was it like a warning of death?

The temples were empty; everybody was at the front or away en route to the mountains. The keepers of the palaces were at the front, helping in whatever task they could manage. The priests kept steady prayers, asking for mercy, constantly scanning the heavens looking for signs of better news. All was gloom. The sages kept finding Venus, the morning star, day by day even closer to the sun, ushering even more bad omens. Not a single shred of hope was present. The odds kept multiplying against the K'iche Empire. It all pointed to a gigantic cosmic conspiracy maybe hatched by the angry dwellers of the sky or the lord of the underworld, Xibalbá.

The predictions made before were reviewed again and again, looking for a clue, a sign that maybe they had missed. But no, all the symbols, all the indications were aligned against them. The predictions were confirmed once, then again and again, immutable, incontrovertible, unchanged.

Ah Puch Kisin, the priest supreme, was even reviewing the predictions made as far as five hundred years into the future, the year 2012 of the

Gregorian calendar, close to 6132 Venus cycles in the long Maya calendar. Every sign was bleak.

Inexorably, he would have to confirm the bad news to his Nima Rajpop Achij. He was afraid of his master's reaction to the dire news. Would he accept the omens graciously or would he explode in a fury against the messenger? Silently he asked for guidance from Tojil, the jaguar god. The priest piously punctured his penis in sacrifice, offering his blood in penance, asking for deliverance for his beloved kingdom. He cried tears of despair. He had never in his whole life been confronted with such bad distress, such overwhelming sorrow. He felt so impotent to bring better news to his lord. He reviewed his life, his actions; maybe he had committed a sin against the gods for which his people were about to be punished. Had he been derelict in his duties as supreme priest? Had he somehow offended his gods?

He had asked more than once the advice of his peers, who could not pinpoint any offenses. Finally, summoning all his courage, he went in search of his master, Lord Tecúm, the Nima Rajpop Achij, to impart the bleak news. In his haste, he forgot while walking to bend his head to avert any offense to the wind god.

Chapter 33

JULY 24, 1524

The troops of the K'akchiquels, commanded by Acajal, and the forces of the Tz'utujils, under the leadership of Xahil, were waiting for the army under Alvarado at the outskirts of the Olintepeque Valley, near the river of the same name. Altogether they numbered close to ten thousand men.

Pedro de Alvarado, the harbinger of destruction and death, with his soldiers, cannons, harquebuses, horses, mastiffs, Tlaxcala and Choluteca Indians, came shortly afterward. He had been a couple of miles downrange, just waiting for his allies to arrive. He didn't want to be seen as needy, begging for the aid of his minions. When he was told by his scouts that the two caciques had arrived, he moved his army and came to their encounter shortly afterward, his pennant floating freely in the soft breeze of the morning. Alvarado was wearing his recently buffed breastplate, polished to a gleam. Trotting at his side as always was his mastiff, Valor, silent, alert, his powerful paws pounding the earth, oblivious to the unfolding drama, eagerly awaiting his master's commands. Its eyes were constantly scanning the scene, its nose identifying the many scents of the hundreds of men, sweat, fear, anticipation.

When Alvarado reached the camp of the two traitorous caciques, he dismounted his mare, Corazón, and started walking to meet the dignitaries. When he was close enough, he saluted the caciques with imperious pomp, addressing them in his halting Maya language, "Nima Acajal, Nima Xahil," he said unctuously, "in the name of our king of Spain, I welcome both of you to our side, to our fight. Now you have the opportunity to avenge all the humiliations you have suffered at the hands of the despicable K'iche armies," he added after spitting on the grass with disdain. He kept going, fueling the animosity these chieftains and their people had against their neighbors the K'iche.

"Together, we can teach your enemies a lesson; punish them for the many offenses they have inflicted on your peace-loving nations." Alvarado continued piling niceties, his captive audience looking at their new master with undisguised envy.

After a while, Xicotenga, Doña Luisa's father, acting as interpreter, continued the translation since Alvarado's limited knowledge of their language had lost impetus. When Alvarado had first advanced, he had removed his helmet to display his golden mane, knowing very well the psychological effect it had on the Indians. It was shining in the morning sun, making the waiting warriors gasp with admiration. They believed they were watching Tonatiuh, the sun, the one god they had been expecting for many generations, the myth reinforced by the oral traditions.

Once the pleasantries and salutations were out of the way, Alvarado went to the root of the problem, his predicament, the *zanjas* his adversaries had dug almost overnight. They were the thorn in his side, the factor that could derail his plans.

"Nima Acajal, Nima Xahil, my scouts had informed me that the enemy had dug deep *zanjas* that will prevent my horses and your people from crossing unimpeded the shallow parts of the river." He made a short pause, gathering his thoughts, trying to find the words to sugarcoat his coming request, the heart of his dilemma. "I need your brave warriors to again fill those trenches so my horses can move freely and punish those rebels. *Por favor* (please) order your warriors to carry out my request without delay. We cannot waste any more time, the day is rapidly advancing." He humbly closed his appeal and departed to join his own forces, internally praying that the two caciques would be foolish enough to order their people to carry a mission tantamount to suicide. Alvarado knew that he desperately needed the aid of these savages; otherwise, his well-laid plans might be derailed. Nevertheless, he rode with a stiff lip, pretending otherwise. He had become a master of appearances and deception.

After a short discussion, the two chiefs commanded hundreds of his troops to carry on the ghastly mission; they were eager to show Alvarado how brave they were. They wanted so much to please their new master, not knowing that he was merely using them for his own sinister purpose; the two chieftains were mere pawns in Alvarado's plans, flotsam that would be cast away as soon as their usefulness was tapped out. They were ignorant that when the battle was over, they would become slaves, laborers to be used in the coming enterprises of the Spaniards. Alvarado, aided by the cunning of Portocarrero, had already devised a plan to distribute the land among his most trusted soldiers.

The planners believed the booty to be gained would be large, enough to pay the troops the salary they were owed, as well as fill their pockets with the gems and gold that supposedly was waiting for them in the palaces and temples of the city they planned to ransack as fast as the enemy could be slaughtered.

As soon as the K'akchiquel and Tz'utujil forces moved to perform their assignment, the attacking forces, once they were within range of the K'iche soldiers, were met by deadly volleys of arrows and *bodoques*, those lethal clay pellets. The defenders had the advantage of the slightly higher elevation of the ramparts, which somehow protected them from the arrows and *bodoques* also used by the advancing armies.

Despite initial heavy losses, the aggressors persisted in their grisly endeavor, fueled by years of enmity and rancor, trying, with the help of the Spaniards, to finally vanquish their most hated enemies, the K'iche. The fatalities kept mounting dramatically, but regardless of heavy casualties, the *zappers* persisted in their quest, sending wave after wave of irate fighters, enraged beyond reason for a cause that was not theirs but the Spaniards, who duped them.

The *zanjas* were rapidly filling with hundreds of dead and the many wounded, their bodies constantly spilling blood and gore, like a gothic spigot that was out of control. The beastly push continued, with more and more men succumbing to the deadly defenders' onslaught. The K'iche warriors were taking advantage of the elevated positions they occupied atop the earthen ramps.

The *bodoques* were decimating the advancing forces with lethal accuracy; the arrows released from the bows of the defenders were adding to the number of fallen aggressors. There were so many wounded, dead, or crippled soldiers that the trenches were rapidly filling with corpses, gore, urine, sweat, dirt, and discarded equipment.

Dozens of warriors were somehow able to find purchase in the ramparts impeding their advance toward the river and were soon escalating them to shortly be repulsed or killed by the K'iche defenders. But the attackers persisted with renewed vigor and were before long engaged in hand-to-hand combat with the men manning the parapets, threatening to overwhelm their resistance.

In the meantime, many of Alvarado's soldiers, spurred by pride or foolishness, had come closer to the newly filled *zanjas* and were promptly engaged in the battle. On seeing this, fast, without delay, Alvarado ordered his *ballesteros* to let loose their lethal short metallic arrows, wounding or outright killing dozens of K'iche warriors who were not aware of this lethal weapon that had a longer range than their antiquated bows and arrows. It became a real massacre, almost a turkey shootout. It was as if death was raining on the defenders. The cannons and some enterprising fusiliers joined the action, releasing volley after volley of unmerciful fire.

The thunder of the cannons and the harquebuses took the hapless K'iche warriors by surprise; they had never encountered such devastating weapons. The carnage was incredible. The blood and urine of so many wounded or dead was soon soaking the grass and the dirt, making the terrain extremely slippery, so much so that the fighting men were having a hard time standing up, loosing balance, slipping in the mire, making completely impossible to release their weapons with any accuracy. Neither band could use the *hondas* with the *bodoques*. The two armies had gotten so close that they had no space to release their projectiles.

The bodies began piling up on both sides; the artillery continued pounding the ramparts, trying to open gaps that would allow the fighters to penetrate the enemy lines. The harquebuses kept firing, filling the air with the pungent smell of burnt powder, adding more noise to the already loud landscape. The Spaniards kept pushing, encouraging their allies with gross imprecations that they could not understand, but even so, they still could grasp the menace implied behind the words.

Pretty soon, the horses were able to negotiate some of the filled sections of *zanjas*, forcing the K'iche soldiers to fall back to their second line of defense across the river. The retreating K'iche were having a difficult time withdrawing, slipping in the wet grass, while being pummeled by the heavy bombardment and the relentless advance of the horsemen who were using their long pikes with deadly dexterity, many men also using their long swords, slashing heads, torsos, raised hands or any exposed parts of the bodies of the defenders. In the confusion, many of the Spaniards' allies were slaughtered since to the Europeans, in the heat of battle, they looked the same as the K'iche.

With a supreme effort, most of the K'iche men reached their new positions and immediately deployed to renew the fight. The blood spilled was so copious that shortly it began running toward the river, staining the waters a crimson red.

The charnel in both sides was atrocious. Thousands of Indians were maimed or dead, while very few Spaniards had perished in the fight.

The K'akchiquel and the Tz'utujil caciques were fuming, furious, loudly complaining that their Spaniard allies were not carrying their part in the fight. Together, Acajal and Xahil went looking for Alvarado, who was watching the battle from a safe distance, to vent their grievances. When Alvarado saw the two caciques advancing, his face briefly contorted in anger but soon assumed his most diplomatic persona and went to meet the advancing chieftains. Without dismounting his mare, he listened with feigned attention to their complaints and halfheartedly promised to order his soldiers to become more active in the struggle. Alvarado was livid with rage. How could these two savages ask him to expose his soldiers? But he pretended to sympathize with the begging caciques.

The two indians generals were slightly mollified but kept their stoic faces, masking their true feelings, not showing any emotion, but inside they were boiling, wondering about the heavy price they were paying for the privilege of being allied with the white devils. They felt betrayed, taken for a ride, a loop that did not bring honor to their people who were lying wounded or dead in the field. The two caciques asked themselves why they didn't pay attention to the offer of Tecúm but persisted on their misplaced belief that Alvarado would lead them to glorious victories and large bounty. They so much desired to come back to K'umarkaj as victors, to reclaim the heritage and prestige that once was theirs, or so they believed.

Alvarado, for his part, was not happy at all with this rebuke. After properly reassuring the bellicose caciques, Alvarado went in search of his captains and ordered them to fake an attack on the weakest flank of the K'iche, with the idea of forcing the enemy to commit more troops to the sector being threatened, therefore easing the pressure on his allies. He was trying to placate his cronies and maybe make the K'iche troops to commit to an action that would destroy their hopes for a victory. His devious mind was changing plans as the battle developed, making adjustments to his strategy. He knew that his tactics were far superior to the obsolete ways of the K'iche warriors. He finally realized, with great satisfaction and surprise, that the defenders didn't have cannons, horses, and dogs.

He was eagerly waiting for the most propitious moment to release those devilish monsters, the mastiffs. Alvarado was sure these beasts would wreak havoc when they charged. On purpose, the day before, the hounds were deprived of food to make sure they would be hungry and eager to attack. The Spaniards had learned this trick when they used the mastiffs against the troops of the moors back in Spain with horrendous results.

The battleground was covered by hundreds of corpses, already decomposing in the heat of the day, their sightless eyes looking at the empty heaven, the sky that once was their pride when they contemplated the stars during the summer months.

Chapter 34

"Kakupatak," Tecúm, the Nima Rajpop Achij, said, addressing his war chief, "the Spaniards are attacking our flanks. Take some men and try to block their advance. For now I will keep the pressure in this sector. Hurry up, move fast. We cannot let the aggressors outflank our troops."

The war chief left with a large contingent of troops, and soon enough he found himself and his men under heavy bombardment, which had started as soon as he left his emplacement. The Spaniards manning the cannons, alerted by Cristobal Olid, the artillery man, saw the forces of Kakupatak moving downrange, rapidly advancing, trying to prevent their defenses from been breached. The invaders were happy to see that the defenders had fallen for the trap and promptly took advantage of the enemy's costly mistake. The pounding was relentless, inflicting heavy casualties to the ranks of the K'iche attackers.

In few minutes, Kakupatak's losses were mounting alarmingly. Despite this butchery, he was able to ward off the attack. He didn't know or suspect that the idea behind this contrived charge was to lure as many of his troops as was possible away from the main line of pressure to allow the K'akchiquels and the Tz'utujils to charge with better chances for success. When this happened, Alvarado and his men fell back to their originally assigned positions; they had accomplished their objective. The enemy had been bloodied really badly. Hundreds of K'iche warriors were lost in this fake attack.

Alvarado was elated; his trap had worked better than he had expected. He had inflicted heavy losses to the enemy. He could now ask his allies to continue their task of trying to penetrate the K'iche defenders, who were resisting valiantly, giving their best in the fight, but finding themselves almost overwhelmed by the brutal bombardment, the almost uninterrupted discharges of the harquebuses and the occasional charge of the horsemen.

The intense fight continued for hours, with partial victories for both sides. The smell of hot blood, urine, dung, and fearful sweat was heavy, permeating the air. The sun was fast setting, lending the battlefield an air of desolation, despair, sorrow, with the constant crying of the wounded or the dying.

The *zopilotes* (vultures) were already circling overhead, patiently waiting their turn to rip apart the corpses strewn in the battlefield. The coppery stench of blood was becoming more noticeable. The river, with so many dead bodies, slowed its course, allowing the waters to pool, tinged with blood, lending the stagnant waters a crimson hue, which was fast enlarging, becoming like a dark mantle that threatened to cover the entire river.

When darkness fell and nobody was able to see the enemy to continue the fight, an undeclared truce was called for the remainder of the day.

It was a moonless night. The only sound heard were the wrenching cries of the wounded, the crippled, or the dying men on both sides, clamoring for relief, many calling their mothers' help. The toll in human lives had been exorbitant in both camps.

Alvarado's men were wiped out, exhausted, beyond tired, encumbered by the heavy *coraza*, greaves, and helmet that with the heat had become a portable furnace, which many men had already discarded, disregarding the danger of the lethal *bodoques*, those infernal clay pellets the Indians were so accurate in delivering. Many were fatally maimed.

The veteran Spaniard soldiers could not believe the ferocity and determination of the K'iche defenders; they were amazed at the cunning they had displayed and grudgingly awarded them, as fellow soldiers, some respect for having paid a heavy price in defending their grounds.

Under the cloak of darkness, with the greatest silence—nobody wanted to become the latest target of the enemy—the dead Spaniard soldiers were removed from the field by their comrades and carried back to their lines, where, with great respect and solemnity, they were buried by their friends. Alvarado, despite his shortcomings, did love and respect his soldiers. With great gravity, he said few words in memory of the fallen, extolling their virtues, lauding the unsolicited sacrifice they had made for the homeland, but he conveniently forgot to mention that they were mercenaries, far removed from any patriotic duty and only looking after their own interest and advancement.

The clerics offered a brief mass in their honor, entrusting their immortal souls to their merciful God, asking in their names for forgiveness, to spare them the torments of purgatory and hell, though they omitted the fact that many soldiers were nonbelievers, that their only god was rapine.

The mood was somber; many men had lost lifelong friends, comrades of many previous wars they had fought together. Alvarado and the clerics knew the names and dreams of some of the deceased men. Sorrow descended on the Spaniard camp. Dozens of victims would never see their lands or their families again. They had died as poor as when they started the invasion, their lives lost in pursuit of ephemeral riches and fame. Many soldiers had not expected to lose their lives at the hands of fighters they considered inferior because they did not look or talked like them; they have paid with their lives for this fatal misconception.

The K'akchiquels and the Tz'utujils, for their part, were unable to recover hundreds of their fallen peers because they were indistinguishable from the K'iche warriors. In silence, with stoicism, they accepted the sad fact that many would not be buried according to the traditions of their ancestors, with the honor and pomp a fallen warrior deserved. They could not even light a funeral pyre for fear of presenting an easy target to the K'iche enemy, watching them from across the waters of the river, who were eagerly hoping for the least mistake on their part. The K'iche warriors were patiently waiting, hoping to catch the enemy unawares.

Nima Acajal and Nima Xahil said few silent prayers for their brave and loyal warriors, entrusting their souls to their gods, wishing them safe passage to the afterlife, hoping they would be spared the torments of Xibalbá, the netherworld.

The night promised to be long and dismal, dark. No *fogatas* (bonfires) were lit. They were afraid of snipers lurking in the shadows. Nobody wanted to become the latest casualty.

Every mind was filled with the uncertainty of the next day. They knew that a more ferocious attack would come at dawn. By now many knew how brave and merciless the K'iche warriors had been. The invaders were not looking at an easy victory.

A brave and lonely Spaniard priest was walking among the men, consoling them, giving spiritual support, blessing the hands and the weapons that next day would kill their brothers! Maybe the cleric didn't know or accepted that God had no favorites or that this conflict was but only an infinitesimal event in the great scheme of the gods. The whimpering of the wounded could be heard in both camps, carried afar by the open space of the valley, a plateau that became the grave for hundreds of warriors, some lost in pursuit of vengeance, others searching for glory to repay ancient feuds. The priest Juan Godinez was, without knowing, silently praying in Latin, oblivious to the fact that his fellow Spaniards didn't understand the universal language of the Catholic Church.

His advance was hampered by the lack of light. He was fully aware that Pedro de Alvarado had forbidden any kind of light that could give away their position. His gentle mind could not understand the reason of the conflict. His soul rebelled at the stupidity of his fellow men. He briefly raised his eyes to the sky and asked God for forgiveness in the name of his flock. The rest of the soldiers were trying to rest, to recover from the day's ordeal. They had to be ready for the coming day. The sound of the waters from the river had ceased, their free flow curtailed by the many corpses floating one on top of the others, forming a tapestry of stiff bodies, entrails, discarded equipment, cannonballs, lances, bows, and a few shields.

Chapter 35

Inspecting his camp, Tecúm, Nima Rajpop Achij, was saddened to see so many of his heroic men slain by the devastating weapons of the Spaniards. He was especially furious with the despicable K'akchiquels and Tz'utujils for lending themselves to be used by the aggressor Alvarado. He had expected that they would see reason and come to his way of thinking, join forces with him and together defeat the Spaniards. Tecúm still could not comprehend why they had allied themselves with the foreigners with whom they had nothing in common. His heart was broken, but his soul was calm, full of purpose, the defense of his homeland.

His mind, for an infinitesimal second, considered the possibility of defeat, but he immediately put that dark thought aside. He could not fail! He had to prevail! All were counting on him.

He ordered a detachment of his men to recover as many corpses as was possible without unnecessarily exposing or exhausting themselves. A huge funeral pyre was lit to cremate those braves fallen defending their sacred land. They would be incinerated according to the Maya tradition, with full honors as a heroic soldier deserved. He thought with sorrow that, given the battlefield conditions, the bodies could not be properly cleaned and purified for the trip to the beyond, as was mandated in the sacred book, the codex that recorded all their traditions, the Popol Vuh, the book of the mat.

The priests were in attendance to offer comfort to the living and to invoke safe passage of the souls of the dead warriors to the waiting arms of Awilix, their god, waiting for them in the heavens. The priests were sure that their immortal souls would ascend to the heavens and become, as tradition stated, shining stars that would send their bright light down to earth. General Tecúm had also ordered to recover as much materiel as his men could find and carry. The supplies were getting lower despite the large quantity of weapons they were able to accumulate in the few days before the battle.

The darkness of the night was disconcerting, full of disquiet calm, an unknown fate still to come the next day. Hundreds of his men had passed to the afterlife. Few could remember a darker night.

Tecúm mulled his predicament, made worse by the fact that many sections of the *zanjas* had been filled again with hundreds of corpses and dirt churned by the incessant bombardment of the cannons. The trenches were no longer of any practical use. Now some horses could negotiate the gaps in the ramparts and roam at will, bringing death to his men. He saw so many of his troops been trampled by the beasts' hooves. He could still hear in his mind the sickening sounds of the heads being crunched under the horses' legs. His mind still reeled at the grotesque spectacle.

Nima Tecúm knew that the Spaniards would again attack in the morning, more determined, encouraged by this early blooding of his troops. He continued asking himself if they should abandon their present positions and move to the city to keep the fight in the streets and the surrounding ravines or, maybe even better, run to the mountains to continue the fight from there, using to their advantage the woods they knew so well.

Tecúm reasoned that if they abandoned their present positions and ran to the *cerros*, they would leave the city wide open, and they would have no home to come back to in case they were victorious. Besides, the city had no walls to ward off any attackers; it was a completely open metropolis. His mind kept revolving on this puzzle, analyzing solutions that could give them some hope for victory.

He ordered to post extra sentinels in strategic points to avoid any surprise night attacks.

Shortly afterward, Kakupatak and his aide-de-camp, Ixpiyacoc, approached Tecúm. They had also been inspecting the outer perimeter of their defenses. They had been happily surprised to find that they had inflicted heavy casualties to the enemy, many more than they had expected or hoped for despite the superior tactics and firepower of the aggressors.

When Nima Tecúm learned about this news, his spirit was lifted. He became more ebullient, more optimistic. Maybe not all was as bleak as it looked. Was it, against all odds, still possible to prevail?

After a light meal, a new strategy was discussed. The war chief spoke, "Nima, I recommend we stay here to continue fighting the enemy the way we are doing now. We had made giant strides in stopping the advance of the Spaniards in their first charge." He continued, "Early morning we will again position our best archers and the ones with *hondas* atop the ramparts from which they can inflict the most number of fatalities to the moving forces. I have seen firsthand the deadly delivery of their *bodoques*, which had accounted for hundreds of casualties."

Nima Tecúm was pensive for a while, analyzing this recommendation that made perfect sense, then he said, "I agree with your proposal, that is our best hope of defeating the assailants." He proceeded, "There are a few more ideas I would like to discuss with you both. I would like to again send a few men to the rear of the enemy and try to kill as many horses and dogs as they can. This may deprive the Spaniards of their *nahuals*. If we can accomplish this, we will take away from them their best offensive weapons, especially those horses."

After a few minutes of reflection, both men almost simultaneously exclaimed, "It is a good idea. Certainly we will not lose anything in trying." So it was agreed to send a band of marauders to harass the rear echelons of the Spanish army.

Ixpiyacoc volunteered to lead a detachment of fighters to do what the plan called for. It was close to suicide, but in the same breath it was worth dying for, protecting their soil.

The leaders kept discussing further plans. They were somehow reluctant to sacrifice such beautiful animals like the horses, though they had no compunction in disposing of the mastiffs, those vicious brutes. The main problem was how to approach undetected. The hellish creatures seemed to possess, besides their keen noses, a sixth sense. At the end, the plan was approved; the daring men would leave before sunrise, in the early hours when they hoped the guards would be half asleep.

Tecúm, the Nima Rajpop Achij, Kakupatak, his war chief, and their aides-de-camp were exhausted, spent, after moving back and forth pushing their troops to fight with honor, with desperation.

They had been everywhere. They sat down to eat a light meal of dried beef, corn tortillas and gulped it down with water from the especially positioned *tecomates (gourds)* along the battle lines Their bodies were covered with dried blood, dust, sweat, and fear, wondering what the new day would bring. Since they were stoic men, no one uttered a word, afraid to betray their misgivings, though each one knew that his friends were of the same mind.

Chapter 36

Prince Tecúm and his friend Ixpiyacoc were sitting side by side reminiscing about the old times, the time they were still carefree, unencumbered by this huge responsibility. Each man wanted to confide in the other, discharge his soul, find solace in the mutual understanding, but somehow they were reluctant to open up, to bare their feelings. It was so hard to talk about personal matters.

"Finally I told K'etzalin about my love for her," Ixpiyacoc told his best friend and commander, Tecúm. "As it happened, she also has the same feelings for me. I even kissed her on the mouth. It was so sweet. I was really surprised after all this years to at last find out that I'm loved back. Ahau, I cannot believe I was such a fool to keep delaying telling her my secret love for her." He took a short breath and continued, "I promised her that one day, soon, I would ask her mother and you, her new father, for her hand. I want to make her my bride and then my wife."

Ahau Galel was so happy for his friend. With sincerity he expressed his best wishes for both and softly, in a manly way, squeezed his friend's shoulder. They kept talking for some more time. Foremost in their minds was the memory of Vukub, the dear friend they had lost a few days before. They could still not reconcile the memory they had of their friend with the grizzly way he was killed by the Spaniard. They really missed him! The friends continued shooting the breeze for some more time, trying to prolong their mutual company. Deep in their hearts they knew that this could be the last time they would talk.

When the time for Ixpiyacoc to depart came, the brothers, with weighty hearts, said their good-byes, their voices choked with emotion. Both were wondering if they would ever see each other again, but they kept a straight face. Life had placed so many demands on their young shoulders; they were barely kids. They had not asked for this burden, but they knew that their nation was the last obstacle standing in the way of the invading

Spaniards. In silence they both prayed to Jacawitz, the patron of their city, to protect them, to endow them with strength and honor, to grant them the means to defend their boundaries against the overwhelming forces facing their nation.

With a final short embrace, they parted company at the outermost side of their lines, Ixpiyacoc walking toward an unknown fate, Tecúm back to the planning and execution of the defense of the city, the metropolis he so much loved, the cradle of his ancestors. From the valley he could see the imposing temples dedicated to his gods to whom he silently prayed, asking them to come to their rescue, invoking their protection in the battle that would come the next morning.

Across no-man's-land, the whining and neighing of the horses mixed with the guttural growls of the mastiffs, which were restless, awaiting the orders of their masters. The soldiers spoke in hushed tones, barely audible, some openly complaining of the smell of the dead. The fusiliers were cleaning their weapons, making ready for next day. They were proud of the way they had handled themselves attacking in an orderly way, paying attention to the orders of their squad leaders.

Chapter 37

The infiltrators had, again, coated themselves with the proven cloak of the castor oil (ricin), shoeless to make them quieter. The only weapons they carried were their obsidian knives, lances, and their *hondas* with plenty of *bodoques*. They had eaten a light meal before departing and had brought with them some rations of *cecina*, fruits, and corn tortillas, food that would sustain them for few days in case they were trapped behind the enemy lines. They were commanded by Ixpiyacoc and were moving like ghosts through the night, concealing themselves in the low mounds and the short grass of the valley. The party had taken a long, circuitous route and approached the enemy camp from the back.

Like thick clay, the hours were dragging slowly, the tension building swiftly. They were wary of the mastiffs. Despite the chill of the night, their skin was covered with a fine layer of perspiration, their sweat helping to increase the release of the pungent odor of ricin, which so far had cloaked them from the mastiffs and the enemy troops.

Now that he had finally professed her love to K'etzalin, Ixpiyacoc was wondering when he would see her again. Her face kept intruding in his thoughts, sweet, open and trusting. He wondered why he had been so slow in realizing that she also loved him. He berated himself for being so dim-witted. Now she was away headed for the sanctuary of Zaculeu. But would she make it? Was she afraid? He wanted so much to be at her side to comfort and protect her and the rest of the family. His mind was really busy with her memory that he found himself not paying attention to his mission. He berated himself when he realized his mistake.

At some point, during the insertion, they would have to slither in the grass, trying to be as silent as serpents. The long years spent hunting deer were coming in handy. After a long, risky time, they reached their intended destination.

Unknown to the intruders, Alvarado had also sent his own group of commandos with two mastiffs accompanying them. The hounds were creeping soundlessly, sniffing the air, trying to identify the scent they had previously encountered. Their leashes had been removed to allow them free reign. Their jowls were dripping saliva, their breath misting in the coolness of the night. Their eyes were wide open, trying to compensate for the poor light of the evening. Time seemed to be moving in slow motion, the senses of all the parties enhanced by the smell of danger. The soldiers' skin released a ripe odor of sweat, fear, and uncertainty despite their experience.

Both contingents were moving in the same direction, getting closer and closer one to each other. The dogs had a tremendous advantage over the humans with their superbly developed sense of smell and their slightly better night vision than their prey, who were unaware of their proximity.

One of Ixpiyacoc's men was poised to deliver his lethal missile when, suddenly, a powerful jaw clamped his arm, almost ripping it with a fierce tug. The warrior, in his surprise, howled with all his might, holding his arm, revealing his position. On hearing the piercing cry, the soldiers with harquebuses loosened a withering discharge immediately killing two and severely wounding one more enemy. The surprise attack had failed. All the advantage had been lost. The mastiffs had discovered and attacked them with fury, as if motivated by revenge.

Pretty soon the scene became chaotic when both bands engaged in hand-to-hand combat, with the upper hand going to the Spaniards with their long swords that allowed their owners to reach their opponents with greater ease. Their training was also proving to be a tremendous advantage. The K'iche warriors were at a disadvantage with their shorter knives and their *hondas*, unable to release the lethal *bodoques* because of the close quarters.

With all the noise going on, the whole camp was immediately awake, with more soldiers joining in the fight. The slave Indians were hiding as best as they could. They didn't want to die in a foreign land unwillingly serving their masters. They were still hoping to one day return to their homes free of the oppressors.

The rest of the mastiffs were released and swiftly joined in the action, maiming or outright killing many K'iche. The beasts had a field day, making a bloody mess of their prey, ripping arms, hands, legs, feet, ears, or any other body part within reach of their powerful jaws. Most of the surprised warriors were terrified, frozen with panic. It was their first battle encounter with these ghastly creatures. Despite their fright, they quickly reasserted themselves, soon returning blow by blow against the Spaniards. Even with their best and concerted efforts, many K'iche were soon wounded, killed, or captured.

Ixpiyacoc was killed by the sword at the hands of Pedro Portocarrero, one of Alvarado's trusted captains, his chest pierced completely. The blood was pouring like a waterfall, draining his life in a few short minutes. Darkness descended on his mind.

The death of Ixpiyacoc was so quick that he didn't even had time to think of his beloved K'etzalin, the love of his life. His body crumpled to the floor and was immediately ripped to pieces by the powerful jaws of the mastiffs that were in a feeding frenzy.

Of the whole party of saboteurs, only one solitary warrior escaped, fast melting into the nearby forest, using the gloom of the night as his cover. Despite his wounds, he was determined to reach the capital and warn his master, Ahau Galel, Nima Tecúm. He was able to reach the river and by waddling in it, by pure luck, was able to lose the mastiffs that were eagerly looking for prey. With a startle, he realized that he had been wounded on his left arm; the cut was a big gash that was bleeding profusely, making him weak with the loss of blood. With great effort, he bent down and took a glob of clay from the riverbed and applied it to the wound, making pressure. After a few minutes, to his amazement and relief, he discovered that the blood had congealed. He took a brief respite, drank the freshwater until his stomach hurt with the large amount that he had swallowed. Once he was sure that the mastiffs had lost his trail, he decided to rest until the morning, settling down in a small bog close to the river.

When dawn came, he set out for the city. He still had to be really careful with his movements; he was not yet out of the proverbial woods. He stayed in the stream for several miles until he was sure enough distance was put between him and those creatures from hell. They were so ferocious, strong, and mean, terrifying in their silent approach.

He was so sad at the loss of his friends, especially at the slaying of his superior Ixpiyacoc at the hands of that beastly Spaniard. How was he going to tell his Nima Rajpop Achij, Tecúm that his best friend was dead, skewered by that tall soldier that he had seen before when he came to the city of K'umarkaj as emissary of his master, Tonatiuh; was he Pedro de

Alvarado? He could not exactly remember the name of the chief of the aggressors. In his mind he thought this was completely irrelevant given his predicament. His main goal was to escape, run for the capital. He had a mission!

Chapter 38

*D*espite his wound, the lonely survivor took to the road, trotting the miles, one after the next and every step taken turning his wounded arm a live torment until he finally reached the outskirts of the metropolis. On seeing him, the sentinels posted rushed to grab him, supporting his weight so he would not collapse. Immediately the warrior was taken to the see their superior in charge.

When the officer came, the escaped combatant kneeled with great effort and spoke in a grave voice, full of pain, sorrow, and shame at being the lone survivor of his team. In a deep voice full of regret, he told the officer that Ixpiyacoc was dead, killed in action by one of the Spaniards. As soon as the superior learned the fate of Ixpiyacoc, one of the best friends of his supreme commander, without delay he ordered two of his soldiers to accompany the injured man to see the Nima Rajpop Achij. The officer was saddened at this news because he was familiar with the deceased fighter and knew that the Nima Tecúm loved him like a brother.

When the wounded soldier approached his supreme commander, with great effort he tried to kneel, but he was prevented from doing this by the Nima, who asked him what happened. With a trembling voice due to his pain, the soldier exclaimed, "Nima Rajpop Achij, I'm sorry to tell you that your friend Ixpiyacoc is dead, he was butchered by one of those foreigners."

With some silent encouragement from the commander, he continued, "Our party was taken by surprise by those ferocious dogs that came out from nowhere. They attacked us with fury, maiming some of the men in our party. Many of the Spaniard soldiers opened up with their 'thunder sticks,' wounding many more of our party. Then, the devils charged us with their long 'knives,' one of them killing your friend Ixpiyacoc." He made a supreme effort gathering his thoughts and continued, "My heart grieves with yours, my Nima, because I know how much you loved your friend."

The rest of his report was sketchy because in the confusion he had not seen much and was lucky to be alive, although he was still very much ashamed.

Ahau Galel, Nima Rajpop Achij, Prince Tecúm, ordered one of his aides to take the man to be attended by the priests, which were versed in war injuries. Ahau had seen that the wound was severe. In a subdued voice, full of grief, he thanked the soldier for his report. Nima Tecúm was devastated. In a short period of time he had lost his best friends, his lifelong companions, one of them his future brother-in-law. What was he going to tell Princess K'etzalin? How would he tell his beloved Ixchel? She was away in the *cerros*, maybe running for her life.

He was fast losing his best friends. He was becoming like driftwood in a raging sea. He could not even mourn his brothers; there was no time. The enemy was knocking at his doors.

After a brief moment, Kakupatak, his mentor and war chief, embraced him like a son and let him vent all his pain, his grief, all his suffering and frustrations.

In a few more minutes, Ahau composed himself and went back to the business at hand, his emotions hidden behind a stoic face. His eyes had become dark, like obsidian, his mind full of resolve. He promised himself that he would not allow the aggressors to seize his land. He vowed to fight them until his last breath.

Ahau, Prince Tecúm, said, "Uncle Kaku, the fight for today is over. I'm sure the enemy would again attack as fast as daylight breaks. Give the order to reinforce the battle stations, make completely sure the men have enough lances, bows, arrows, and *hondas*." Ahau knew with certainty that Alvarado, his nemesis, would charge before the sun was high. "I promise you, I would make the intruder pay for his insolence."

In silence, the prince and his mentor took a light meal, rested for a while, then, with a final embrace, each man went his own way to carry his part in the coming battle. They had agreed to meet later on at a prearranged place in the remaining ramparts. Each man was aware of the role they would play.

Walking the theater of action, Tecúm was looking for weak spots, probing, encouraging his soldiers. With deep sadness he mulled at how young they were, many of them completely unfamiliar with the art of war, away from their families, far from their loved lands, the soil they worked with such dedication and love.

He was so proud that no one complained; they were ready to fight the enemy. Each one had promised to defend their way of life, to try to preserve their traditions and beliefs against such incredible odds. The invaders possessed so many powerful weapons, and they fought with tactics the K'iche warriors were not familiar with. The cannons were devastating. They could hurl big balls of a material they didn't know about that were capable of cutting many men to smithereens, or break apart the ramparts, sending geysers of dirt, body parts, and garments when they impacted with a heavy thud. He would have to keep his soldiers as far away as was possible from these contraptions and the deadly fire sticks that belched fire. But how could he accomplish this and at the same time try to kill or wound the enemy?

Chapter 39

After their rounds were completed, as previously arranged, Ahau Galel, Prince Tecúm, and his war chief, Kakupatak, met at the designated point to wait the few remaining hours of the night. After exchanging impressions and agreeing to the next day's plan of action, each man pretended to fall asleep and every *guerrero* (warrior) was alone with his demons, his dreams and his hopes.

Kakupatak, the war chief, kept mulling the best strategy, kept revising the previous day's battle, analyzing, trying to remember crucial details that could help his principal to be victorious in the coming battle. He had previous battle experience, but it was against their enemies, the K'akchiquels and the Tz'utujils. They were nothing like these foreign devils, these *jolom kiej* (sons of bitches) who came to his lands with those terrible dogs and those huge war steeds, with those loud tubes that belched destruction and death. His mind kept revolving in this conundrum until finally fatigue took over.

Ahau Galel, Prince Tecúm, kept thinking of Ixchel, his lovely betrothed. He knew he loved her with all his heart. She was so full of life, so vibrant, loving, attractive, her regal presence enough to fill a room and make the onlookers dip their heads in wonderment. Ahau knew he was lucky to be loved by such a great woman. What a pity! The events unfolding had forced them to say good-bye. Ahau silently entrusted her to his gods, asking them to grant them the happiness to see each other again.

He was sad thinking that she was alone in the mountains, maybe afraid for her safety, possibly hunted by the enemy. He almost cried aloud but kept his voice under control. He could not show weakness to his men. He was a Maya prince!

Up in the sierras, Ixchel was having the same worries, her mind busy with the memory of their last encounter. She could still feel the kiss they had exchanged, followed by many more in a matter of mere minutes. It had been the very first time they ever kissed on the mouth before getting married, which was against tradition. But how sweet it had been to feel his hot breath on her neck; to relish those strong lips and taste the essence of his desire. To see in his eyes his devotion and his longing, to caress with her hands those powerful muscles, to get to know that she was wanted as much as she wanted him. She knew with utmost certitude that she loved him with all her being.

Ixchel hoped that one day, soon enough, she would again see him and then she would let him know how much she loved him. She promised the sun-god, Kinich Ahau, that when they married, she would be a good wife and would bear with pride his children if the god delivered them from this nightmare. Ixchel could not even talk to her sister, K'etzalin, or to her mother, Ixmucané, for fear of being overheard by the spies that could be lurking in the shadows waiting to capture them because she was positive that by now the aggressors had discovered their escape. Or was it possible that the enemy had paid no attention to the escaping party? Maybe they were busy getting close to the valley, though she could not completely trust those K'akchiquels. Perhaps they were following them, just waiting for an opportune moment to seize her group. She kept pounding the hardened soil, feeling every time her feet met the pebbles like stabs in her heart.

The landscape with no moon was an eerie greenish, menacing, forbidden. *Maybe,* Ixchel thought, *this is what Xibalbá looks like.* The long column was following a path lost in the *cerros*, solitary, unknown but to the hard-core hunters.

Chapter 40

"**P**edro and Cristobal," Pedro de Alvarado commanded his trusted captains Pedro Portocarrero and Cristobal Olid, "come with me; we have to discuss the plan for tomorrow's battle." Alvarado continued, "Cristobal, you will be in charge of protecting the right flank, and you, Pedro, I want you to take care of the left side. In the meantime, I would lead the main attack in the center." Alvarado's sagacious mind had come up with a bold plan that would assure him victory.

Alvarado's aim was to split the K'iche defenders, forcing them to protect three fronts, which would force them to stretch their lines. Alvarado was also thinking in using the cannons and the harquebusiers more effectively now that he knew the K'iche didn't have any firepower. His *ballesteros* would be positioned in a way to kill any K'iche defender that exposed his body's upper part in the ramparts. The Spaniards would be using the now abandoned K'iche ramparts in the now overrun first line of defense.

Part of the *zanjas* could now be crossed with relative ease by the big war horses. The animals would traverse the short no-man's-land to the margins of the river in a few minutes, hoping that the defenders would not defend this area or that they would be fighting in the open, where the horsemen could make mincemeat of the warriors on foot.

All those long hours practicing in the beaches of Cádiz were about to bear fruit. The *jinetes* (horsemen) were eager to show their prowess. They also wanted glory even if it was acquired against almost defenseless foes.

After a few more minutes discussing with his captains, Alvarado went looking for a place to rest for the remainder of the night. Once he was settled, his mind started to wander. Alvarado still could not believe the ferocious resistance the K'iche warriors had put up. He was amazed that the K'iche cacique had almost outmaneuvered him. Who was this man? Alvarado mused. He had no first knowledge of his opponent except the tales he was told by Xahil and Acajal, the K'akchiquel and Tz'utujil chieftains, stories he knew were somehow embellished by these fools trying to justify their defeats in previous wars with the K'iche.

These caciques described Ahau Galel, Tecún, as a powerfully built warrior, cunning and courageous. They had told him that the K'iche cacique, known to them as Tecún Umám, was the grandson of Don K'iqab, the recently slain K'iche king in one of the last wars these kingdoms fought. Their embellishments asserted that Tekún was a god covered with quetzal feathers, which could lift him to the sky. Then, while flying close to the sun and the stars, he would direct his troops against his enemies. These caciques swore that Tekún was protected by his *nahual*, the quetzal, which could render him invisible to the human eye. These men were deadly afraid of the K'iche warriors, which had defeated them so many times before, so they had to exaggerate his skill.

Alvarado was skeptical of this information, but he gave some credence to it based on his own belief that he himself was the reincarnation of the apostle Santiago, who was also capable of flying to the skies riding his horse to bring death and destruction to his enemies. Pedro de Alvarado's mind always conjured the white garments of the saint whose bones were interred in the cathedral of Santiago de Compostela, Spain, a place Alvarado had never in his life visited. Nevertheless, somewhere along his travails, Alvarado had picked the saint as his protector and invoked the saint's name before each battle.

When his mind stopped wandering, Alvarado's mind focused again on practical matters. He lamented about not having any catapults or any assault engines, like those big ballista the Romans had in ancient times that could hurl with ease big rocks against the ramparts of the K'iche. Alvarado vowed to unleash the next day without mercy the fury and savagery of his mastiffs, those beasts that proved to be so efficient in dismembering and killing the enemy troops. He knew the animals were hungry for more blood.

Alvarado was lying down, using the saddle of his horse as a pillow, contemplating the few stars visible in the dark night. His mind kept drifting to Raquel Fuentes, that green-eyed beauty he unwillingly left behind in La Esperanza when he and his brothers ran for their lives. Several years had passed since that fortuitous encounter. Was she still single? he wondered. Did she still remember him?

How many turns his life had taken since that far-away time. He had become a great captain in the service of Hernán Cortés and his king, Carlos V. Now he was a governor! He briefly reminisced about Sara and Alejandro, his uncle, still marveling at their selfless help when they offered the fugitive brothers sanctuary when they came destitute to Cádiz. Pedro could not forget Sara's word of support during his bouts of despondency. How her words had lifted his spirits. He thought that she was akin to an angel.

His mother, Mexia, intruded his mind in the last minutes before he drifted to sleep. Alvarado remembered her beautiful face, her kind words when she caressed him close to her bosom. Was she still alive? Did she receive the last money they had sent her before leaving Cádiz? His mind didn't think about his father or that irascible, drunk priest.

Pedro de Alvarado finally marveled at the fact that despite his youth he managed to influence his older brothers and his cousin Rodrigo Sosa to follow him to come to these lands. Alvarado's last thought was of victory. He knew he would be rich and famous!

Chapter 41

*P*edro Portocarrero was also alone with his memories as a child. He left his home in Zaragoza, Spain, the son of parents of the nobility who were close to the court of the king. He was born rich. He had a promising future, lands he would inherit from his parents since he was the firstborn. He had a name, a title that would be his upon the death of his father, *el Marquéz* (the marquise). Instead he left all that behind and came to Cádiz, where he met Cortés and Pedro de Alvarado.

His wandering soul found a twin soul with Alvarado's, who had convinced him to sail with him to the New World in search of adventure and glory, his own hard-earned glory. He, now in this faraway land, had found more than he had expected to find. Pedro had become Alvarado's right hand, one of his most trusted advisers. Maybe someday he would become a governor of a province or, even better, a viceroy. His last thoughts were of his parents and relatives.

Juan Godinez, one of the priests in the expedition, was fervently praying to his God, asking him to safeguard his flock. He was afraid that the next day would bring more suffering, more destruction and more death. During the day, he had witnessed the fury of the cannons and the harquebuses, which ripped the enemy soldiers to pieces, sending their limbs into the air. He was appalled at the carnage inflicted on the Indians who were fighting for their survival. He could not reconcile this picture with the teachings of his Lord. Somehow he regretted his coming to these unknown lands with the idea to save souls, but instead he had found himself immersed in a bloodbath. Who would he be able to save? The way the onslaught was going, he doubted that any souls would be left to save.

Juan continued with his prayers, his voice lost in the cacophony of the laments of the maimed soldiers. In the morning he would try to convince Alvarado to cease hostilities and forgive the non-existent offenses of the Indians. His mind finally succumbed to sleep, holding in his hands the crucifix, the symbol of another needless tragedy that happened many centuries before.

Juan Argueta for his part was reviewing his obscure life, a life that was nothing before he met Alvarado in Cádiz. Then all his prospects had changed dramatically, becoming, almost overnight, the right hand of the governor, the man Alvarado depended on more and more. He would stick to his master like glue. Maybe in doing so he would be rewarded for his loyal services, maybe even made a captain general, although this would be hard since his proficiency with reading and writing were almost nonexistent. Given his humble origins, he thought he had done pretty good so far.

Chapter 42

JULY 25, 1524

That morning, the sun rose earlier than usual, hot, merciless, illuminating a macabre landscape, charred with the burnt powder, littered with hundreds of dead K'akchiquels and Tz'utujils, mingled with a few Spanish soldiers and one or two dead horses.

The stench of the decomposing corpses was overpowering, lending an air of desolation to the scene. Smoke still drifted from the funeral pyre the K'iche warriors lit the night before to cremate their dead warriors as was the costume. They also numbered in hundreds without including the corpses that were not recovered.

As the wind changed on and off, it brought to the Spaniard camp the sweet, unpleasant smell of burnt bodies and the reminder of near defeat inflicted by those savages!

In some sector, the river had stopped running, the flow impeded by the hundreds of cadavers strewn in it. The water had turned a deep ochre, dirty, with a film of oil from the fluids of the many slain people.

The K'iche warriors awoke early, full of purpose, buoyed by the heavy casualties inflicted to the enemy. Each one silently marched to man their positions. They were ready for their foe. The orders were given in hushed tones since the leaders didn't want to be overheard by the K'akchiquels and the Tz'utujils, who could understand their language, and also as a sign of respect for their departed brethren.

When they went atop the remaining ramparts, the sight across the river froze their hearts; again, the enemy had massed their troops, aided by the imposing horses and those menacing, huge mastiffs. A sort of stunned incredulity overwhelmed their senses. For many of them, it was the very first time they had seen up close such animals. The picture was terrifying.

Even from a distance, the dogs looked so large, mean. The warriors with the acutest vision could see their frothing jaws, dripping saliva, smelling blood, anxious to be let go from their leashes.

The view became more worrisome when they saw the cannons arranged in a single file, facing them, with the soldiers manning them wearing their silver helmet and buffed breastplate. Now they could see that many of them carried the dreaded thunder stick. Many combatants were happy that they still had the river between them and the intimidating assailants.

The K'iche warriors were seething at the despicable K'akchiquels and Tz'utujils, who had joined forces with the Spaniards against them, their neighbors, their own blood, disregarding their common heritage, their common language. It was madness!

They were aware that when the traitorous bastards attacked, it would be without mercy, full of fury, relentless, seeking revenge for the countless defeats they had suffered at the hands of the K'iche. Acajal and Xahil, their leaders, were raving mad, exhorting their troops to avenge their dead, to erase from their collective memory the name of the K'iche.

The presence of the K'akchiquel and Tz'utujil troops loomed large, menacing, covering a vast track of land, with the Spaniards moving among them, giving orders, as if their allies were already their slaves, as if they already owned the land.

The K'iche defenders could hear indistinct voices, giving commands in another language, a language that they could not understand, a language they had never heard before. The voices were coarse, full of epithets, urging their underlings to advance, to attack, taunting the Indians, calling them cowards, laughing at their blank facial expressions when they could not understand a word they were saying despite the translators, who were busily trying to make sense of the orders they were receiving. When the Spaniards realized their allies could not understand most of the orders they were spitting out, they became enraged, almost to the point of attacking their own minions. It was bedlam. The poor interpreters were hard-pressed to carry on the rapid-fire orders as best as they could.

Chapter 43

With a fierce determination borne from hate and desperation, the K'iche defenders set to do their sacred duty, the defense of their homeland. They found themselves alone, betrayed, outnumbered, outgunned and poorly equipped; in tactical military disadvantage. But they were proud, brave, the last direct descendants of the Maya. Many warriors believed that their ancestors were watching from the heavens and would reward them for their bravery.

Many soldiers knew this could be their last day on this earth, but all were eager to engage the enemy, to prove themselves worthy of the trust their Nima Rajpop Achij had bestowed on them. Everyone was proud of their commander, Ahau Galel, Prince Tecún Umám, whom they looked with hope as the savior of their people. They had seen his bravery during the battle of the previous day. They had witnessed their Nima dispensing blows, killing many enemies in his path. He was a giant guiding them. He was a beacon of hope, a light they wanted to emulate and follow.

Despite the fact that they were not a professional army, each soldier was maintaining his composure, silent, mulling his own thoughts. Many soldiers looked with longing at the bluish mountains in the distance, so inviting, so safe and welcoming! How easy would be to escape to that sanctuary, but nobody did. They loved their land; they were proud. They were men of honor!

Nima Rajpop Achij, General Tecún Umám, was moving among his troops, instilling confidence in those wavering, counseling calm, lifting their spirits, prodding those afraid with kind words, sometimes lightly touching them in the back. The mood was solemn; the silence was overwhelming.

Their first line of defense had fallen the day before, and they had quietly and orderly retreated to their second line of defense across the river.

The valley where the armies had clashed the previous day was called Xelahub (place of many quetzals). Overhead many of those beautiful birds could be seen, keeping station, watching the folly taking place below. The sacred birds were displaying their long curved tails, their wings fluttering in the soft wind. Some men with acute eyes could make the deep crimson chest of the birds. Many wondered if this could be an omen of their deliverance since the *nahual* of their prince was the quetzal.

Kakupatak, the war chief, was also walking his positions, making sure his men were ready for the attack, asking them if they had enough *bodoques* and arrows. The answer given was that they had plenty since the night before they had recovered large caches of materiel.

His principal dilemma he had discussed with Tecúm was the lack of experienced leaders that could lead squads of soldiers in the coming assault. He had delegated many soldiers with this task, but he was still not satisfied. Kakupatak knew that when the push came, this experience would be crucial and could turn the tide in their favor. He was a practical man. He would have to make with the resources he had at hand.

He tried to bring to his mind the teachings of his mentor, the great king Don K'iqab, the commander he had admired and tried to emulate most of his life. By Tepeu, the god creator, how he missed that wise man! Now he craved his counsel.

He was sad to see that his first line of defense had been overrun yesterday, but he consoled himself because they had discussed with Ahau this possibility before. So, that was no surprise.

He continued his walk, stopping here and there. At his back he could see his beloved K'umarkaj, the city in which he was born, the cradle of his ancestors. He could appreciate from this far the beauty and symmetry of the temples, but at the same time he could see, as they had seen before, that his capital was wide open, a nightmare to defend if they had to retreat to it. Would he ever see his birthplace again?

Chapter 44

Across the river, in the enemy camp, Pedro de Alvarado y Contreras was moving in the midst of his soldiers, riding his gorgeous black mare, Corazón, moving her through the camp with grace at a sedate pace. Trotting at his side, like a shadow, was Valor, his loyal mastiff, silent but coiled to spring into action at the least indication of his master. The mastiff was an imposing animal, large, with shiny black pelt, now matted with dry blood spilled the day before. His eyes were alert, vigilant, scanning the scene, recording in his retinas the images of friends, looking for enemies, eager to destroy them with his powerful jaws and huge paws.

Pedro de Alvarado y Contreras was reviewing his troops. At times he was joking with the soldiers. At times he was scolding the lazy ones. He was full of purpose. He was a man of imperious will with a singularly bright mind. He was full of confidence and trusted his fighters with whom he had now been together for many years. He had promised his soldiers untold riches, treasures, honor and fame, and in the worst of cases, a glorious death.

Alvarado had already had a mental conversation with the spirit of the apostle Santiago, his self-appointed guardian angel. In Pedro's mind, the angel had assured him of a great victory. Captain Pedro de Alvarado had made his purpose to erase this enemy from the face of the earth, to punish them for the early affront of refusing to bend to his demands for an unjust alliance. He had made this his solemn duty. He would prevail!

His mind was working overtime, mentally moving his forces back and forth, like a giant chess game, adapting new moves when his intellect told him that that maneuver would not work. Alvarado was afraid that the two Nimas Acajal and Xahil would not abide by his orders. He went in search of his cousin Rodrigo Sosa. When he found him, he said, "Rodrigo today is the day we have been waiting for, today all our dreams will come true."

He continued, "make sure that your dog, Amigo, is alert and primed for action because at some point in the battle, I would release the mastiffs, I know the indians are petrified with their presence. Also, when the time comes, I will order the horsemen to attack. Make sure you stick with Olid. He has a lot of experience and can protect you in case you need help."

Alvarado was worried about his cousin, the friend that had been with him for many years now, from his infancy. He really felt a great deal of affection for his cousin. He inquired from Sosa where his brothers were, making sure they were also somehow protected from the main assault. He didn't want to lose them and have to explain to his mother his failure to protect them.

Chapter 45

*J*uan Diaz, one of the clerics, together with Juan Godinez, was conducting his spiritual rounds. Inside he was reminiscing about his natal land, the Canary Islands, the place he left to come to Cádiz, looking for bigger catch of souls, trying to amend the sins of his youth. His parents were devout Catholics and wanted for him to be a priest, one of the few ways in those times a person could accumulate wealth and prestige with more chances of acceptance in a much closed society.

When he arrived in Cádiz, poor, hungry, and lost, by pure chance, he met the bishop, who took him under his wing. Under the bishop's guidance, Juan learned to read and write Latin, the universal language of the Catholic Church, with the addition of some basic Greek. He so much wanted to read the old biblical texts authored by the first followers of Jesus Christ. When the bishop offered him a chance to travel to the New World as his emissary, he jumped at the opportunity of saving the souls of savages that didn't know about the mercy of Jesus. Now he was bogged down in this faraway land, surrounded by angry Indians and deranged Spaniards. He invoked his Lord for protection, for guidance to understand this mockery.

They were moving cautiously among the soldiery, wondering why men were so intent in killing one another. Their kind and gentle souls could not comprehend this abhorrence. The clerics listened to a few men's confessions, gave absolution for the crimes they were about to commit. Some soldiers received communion and were now sanctified to kill the heathens in the name of their Lord.

Many soldiers were wary of the fury of the K'iche. The previous day they had witnessed their determination, amazed at their skill and bravery. They had grudgingly come to respect the zeal with which these men were defending their homeland.

Some soldiers had been brave enough to ask their commander, Alvarado, to spare this gallant people. Some fighters had already seen in action the K'iche warrior they later learned was called Tecún Umám, the Nima Rajpop Achij, the great captain general, fight with great resolve, a bronzed figure, full of passion, might, and purpose. Many soldiers were now afraid to face these warriors. Even in their battles against the Moors back in Spain, they had never encountered braver and more dedicated soldiers.

The invaders had seen firsthand the devastating effect of those damned clay pellets, responsible for the death of many of their comrades. They had never seen those weapons. The eerie sound the slingshots made before the pellet was released was unnerving, like the sound of thousands of locusts approaching, decimating everything in their path.

Some alert foreigners had observed that the enemy soldiers were constantly chewing a soft gooey off-white matter. Later on, questioning their allied K'akchiquels, they were told this stuff was called copal and was extracted from a tree called ramon and sapodilla upon slashing the cortex. On chewing, this material became soft, pliable, produced more saliva, and decreased thirst. Years in the future, the soldiers became addicted to this copal and started shipping it to Spain.

The soldiers observed that the K'iche warriors were lightly dressed, with only a short tunic, like a kilt, around their waist to cover their genitals. Some of the braves wore a light white vest intended to protect their chest. Their feet were clad with sandals with sturdy soles, which the Indians called *caites*. Each K'iche warrior carried a rounded shield made of thick animal hide stretched over a wooden frame, a long lance, several slingshots, and plenty of clay pellets.

They had seen these men move with extreme grace and speed from place to place as ethereal creatures. Few of them wore feathers around their wrists or ankles. Were these men officers? They wondered. Or maybe those feathers gave them extra protection?

Many soldiers were familiar with the long tunics and headgear of the Moors and their long curved scimitars, but this was something new. They had never witnessed semi-naked fighters. What a crazy land this was.

Chapter 46

The tension in both camps was palpable, like thick molasses; the armies were ready to clash. The Spaniards were about to unleash their pent-up fury at these savages. They wanted to kill as many enemies as they could, wishing to open the road to the hoards of gold and gems they were to get. The soldiers looked with longing at the edifices of the city in the distance.

The foreigners were getting closer and closer to the K'iche emplacements. The hell of battle was about to be lit with the cannons and the harquebuses.

The monotonous beat of the many *tuns* of the K'iche, the K'akchiquels, and the Tz'utujils was deafening, the sound alerting the warriors in both sides to prepare for the oncoming assault from the Spaniards and their lackeys. The haunting notes of the *chirimillas* lent a disquieting sound to the scene. The battle was about to begin. History was about to be written with the blood of the innocent. A massacre of epic proportions was about to unfold.

Alvarado commenced his charge by moving some K'akchiquel troops to the right, overseen by Spaniard officers, commanded by Cristobal Olid. On the left flank, the Tz'utujils were supervised by Pedro Portocarrero and Gómez, one of Alvarado's brothers. The Spaniards were there to make sure their allies followed the orders to fight European-style and not revert to their old ways of charging en-masse, in a disorganized way.

Pedro de Alvarado decided to command the center with a select group of soldiers, including Juan Argueta, that drifter Alvarado had picked at Cádiz. He would anchor the charge.

The three columns would move like a solid wall, with precision, trying to get unscathed close to the K'iche defenders. The cannons were placed in strategic positions, close to the advancing columns, from where they could be more effective and inflict the more damage. The only problem, maybe the most crucial for Alvarado's troops, was the river, deep in the sector they were attempting to wade across, for they had to get close to the enemy for their weapons to be effective.

The horsemen were kept slightly in the background, waiting the best time to attack. The horses were restlessly trampling the soft earth, already soft in some areas, thick and gummy, sticky. Once the cannons were within range, all the forty pieces opened fire, hurling large balls directed toward the ramparts, trying to break gaps, which the footmen could use to penetrate the lines of the K'iche defenders. The noise was like thousands of thunder descending from the heavens, the smoke obscuring the dismal valley.

The roar of the opening salvo took the K'iche by surprise since they were not aware of the destructive power of the cannons. Dozens were maimed or outright killed during this early stage of the battle. The destruction was horrendous, sickening and unbelievable.

The air soon became thick with the smoke of the artillery, saturated with the pungent, dry smell of burnt powder.

The pounding was relentless, salvo after salvo. Shortly, a few gaps appeared in the ramparts. Encouraged by this sight, many K'akchiquel and Tz'utujil troops advanced openly but soon found themselves under heavy attack, peppered by deadly arrows and a hail of *bodoques*. Hundreds were killed, littering the field with their bodies, like a tapestry of death.

After the initial barrage, the cannons were primed with grapeshot as to inflict the largest number of casualties to the enemy. The artillery was having a devastating effect on the defending K'iche across the river, their bodies cut to pieces by the deadly projectiles. The carnage was mounting alarmingly, many areas of the ramparts started showing gaps in the defenders' ranks, which by now lay immobile, inert, dead, pulverized.

The mastiffs were still leashed, their jaws foaming at the smell of blood, anxiously tugging at their bounds, urging their keepers to let them go. Their powerful paws were impatiently thumping the earth, ready to smash the enemy.

The next wave in the attack brought the *ballesteros*, which released thousands of short heavy metallic arrows to the skies, aiming for the enemy camp, sowing pain and death when they found their mark. The blood spilled was abundant, draining in geysers from the wounded warriors, increasing more and more as many new men were struck. Some of the blood, after soaking the dirt, was already running toward the river, turning the clay into a thick, slippery reddish mud.

The casualties in Alvarado's camp were also mounting at a rapid pace. Alvarado had purposely sent his indian allies as the first waves of the assault to bear the brunt of the K'iche response. The number of dead was quickly escalating, inexorably, like a river flowing without obstacles in its path.

When the K'akchiquel and Tz'utujil squad leaders realized that their men were dying in large numbers, they started to complain openly, grumbling to their caciques that the number of killed Spaniards was minimal. The Spaniards wisely had stayed safely away from the danger, in the periphery of the battle. The few more daring Spaniards that joined the Indians in the attack found themselves bleeding profusely, maimed or dead. The wounds inflicted by the K'iche arrows were jagged and large due to the heavy uneven surface of the obsidian projectiles. When many Spanish soldiers realized this, they removed themselves from the conflict with loud imprecations. They hadn't enlisted to be caught in this massacre.

The sun kept rising, increasing the heat of the battlefield, accelerating the decomposition of the corpses, with the stench of spilled blood, urine, feces, and sweat making it worse. The grass was becoming more slippery for the soldiers, which were having a hard time keeping their footing to aim with precision.

Hundreds of attackers perished when in a brave gesture they tried to rush the ramparts, which, with the pounding of the cannons, had become loose and unstable, the dirt and the dust adding to the confusion of the arena. With so much blood, it had turned like goo, extremely slippery. For several hours the attackers were unable to gain too much ground, constantly slipping in the mire. The charge continued unabated, slowly decimating the brave K'iche defenders, who stubbornly clung to the last pieces of their land, desperately trying to stay alive. They knew that the K'akchiquels and Tz'utujils would be merciless if they were defeated. No one wanted to become slave to the invaders; they preferred to be dead. They took example in their leaders Tecúm and Kakupatak, who were fighting valiantly.

Chapter 47

The K'iche defenders had availed themselves with courage and determination, inflicting a heavy blow to the initial charge of the enemy, which slowly was losing steam, bogged down in the slippery terrain.

Nima Rajpop Achij, Tecún Umám, the K'iche general, had chosen his defenses with cunning and great care. So far, his plan was on track and holding beautifully against the enemy charge. His soldiers were reaping enormous dividends in fatalities inflicted mostly to his enemies the K'akchiquel and the Tz'utujil. The hated enemy was at least, for the time being, bogged down in massive casualties.

Alvarado was beside himself; furious with this early setback. He could not believe the bravery and resilience of the enemy. He was unable to explain to himself and to his men how a bunch of savages were keeping at bay his better-trained and better-equipped troops. It was preposterous. How was this possible? He wondered.

He was livid with rage, his dark side threatening to sink his plans. He was absentmindedly caressing his mare's mane, trying to calm down, speaking to himself in hushed tones. His noble beast was patiently bearing his weight. His mastiff, Valor, was also quietly awaiting his commands, static, coiled, yet ready to spring at the least hint of his master's desires.

"Cristobal, Pedro, come here fast," Alvarado summoned his trusted captains, Cristobal Olid and Pedro Portocarrero, to an impromptu parley. "I need a diversion right away," Alvarado said. "Olid, you go to the right, and you, Pedro, I want you to go to the left flank," Alvarado continued. "*Tomad los perros* [take the mastiffs] and let them go free when you get close to the enemy lines. Now that some parts of the wall have been breached, it would be easier for them to attack the enemy. Use some of our soldiers in the charge; I don't want any excuses from the men for refusing to join the action. Our allies are already complaining that we are avoiding the fight, letting them carry the burden of the battle," Alvarado said. "Xahil and Acajal are threatening to abandon the clash. If they desert us, we are for sure lost," he explained.

"Argueta, you will ride with me in the center, guarding my left side," Alvarado further ordered the sergeant Juan Argueta.

Pedro de Alvarado continued with his harangue, "The sun is already high in the sky, close to noon. Time is fast slipping away from our hands. There is no more time to waste. Go on, hurry up." With this final admonition, Pedro de Alvarado set his pace for the battle lines, with his faithful dog trotting by his right side, Argueta guarding his left. The mastiff was as usual silent yet primed to act in a flash. His powerful paws moving him closer to the enemy camp. The more they advanced in the field, the more his paws and the hoofs of Corazón got covered with sticky blood, the clip-clop of her movement sounding like a death kernel. The master and his mare were like a unit, moving with coordinated grace, like a deadly ballet dancing to the music of destruction and sorrow.

Alvarado was oblivious to the dozens of *bodoques* and arrows flying around him; he was feeling protected from any harm by the mantle of his patron, the apostle Santiago. Pedro felt bound to fulfill his self-imposed destiny, intent on his own crusade, going against the specific orders that his commander, Hernán Cortés, gave him in the official letter when he had authorized the expedition that Alvarado proposed. Alvarado kept reasoning that once the conquest was completed, Cortés would have to accept it as an accomplished fact and come to terms with it. The consequences be damned! Wasn't he the governor of Oaxaca?

He kept his unrelenting advance, his pennant carried by Argueta, floating freely in the soft breeze, heralding his ego. His mere presence brought renewed joy and encouragement to his men, who worshiped their captain. He was the prophet leading them to the promised land of gems and gold, to new heights of glory and honor.

Silently, as he advanced, his soldiers bowed, saluting him. He looked magnificent, imposing, in his great Andalusian horse, with the huge dark mastiff completing the apocalyptic scene, the harbingers of pain, suffering, and death!

The K'iche warriors, across the river, were quietly, and with trepidation, watching this apparition from Xibalbá. Olid and Portocarrero were carrying his orders with precision, moving with ease atop their huge war beasts, fearless, as if they were also protected by an invisible guardian angel. Rodrigo Sosa was riding shotgun with Portocarrero, while Gonzalo, Alvarado's brother, was at the side of Olid, forming a solid wall of steel. Meanwhile, the two clerics were fervently praying to God to stop this insanity, to avoid more casualties, but apparently the indian gods and the Christian God were deaf to the voices of the humans.

Chapter 48

ave after wave of furious and screaming K'akchiquel and Tz'utujil, with a few Spaniard advisers spurring them, was repulsed by the K'iche defenders, who were fighting with superhuman determination, beyond pain and beyond endurance.

The fatalities kept mounting, the grass and the dirt getting wetter with the spilled blood, urine, and excrement of the wounded soldiers in both sides. The amount was so copious that some areas of the river were getting redder, crimson.

The assault continued, unremitting, with both sides pushing and shoving to gain a few precious meters, to then lose them again in a few minutes. The grunts and lamenting of the combatants were piercing the eerie silence of the valley. Many sections of the short grass was charred by the spent powder, probably dead for generations to come. The sick sound of the swords hitting naked torsos was augmented by the dull thuds of the maces splitting heads.

The mastiffs had been released and were raising havoc, biting, chomping, tearing big chunks of flesh, many times whole limbs, the agony of their victims shouting dreadful cries.

The pain and destruction was ghastly, unbelievable. The victims were terrified of the big monsters, but despite their fright, they continued holding their ground, sometimes fighting the dogs with their bare hands, knowing well that any weakness on their part could mean the end of their kingdom. Hundreds knew they were about to die, that this could be their last moments on this earth, but they persisted in their effort, trusting the afterlife promised to them by their priests.

The K'iche warriors could not waver at this point. Despite overwhelming forces coming their way, the K'iche soldiers kept holding their lines of defense, stopping the hordes of the enemy, negating them an easy victory. Retreat from a sector was ordered only when the defense of that spot became untenable. Only then they moved to another section. The realm was in mortal danger of extinction.

The obsidian-studded clubs were turning into pulp the heads being hit, ending the life of that soldier with a sickening crunch, like fragile eggshells. The *bodoques* were also sending many combatants to the afterlife, piercing the soft parts of the craniums they landed on.

The sun was now on its zenith. The landscape had turned into a grotesque, surreal painting, full of desolation, cries, and the relentless pounding of the horses' hooves.

Tecún Umám was everywhere, encouraging his warriors, maiming or killing his enemies with the powerful swings of his club or the stabbing of his obsidian knife. His body was drenched in blood and sweat. His ornate vest was no longer white; it was now sodden with so much gore. He was unrelenting, pressing his advantage, sensing that his efforts and the effort of his people were carrying the day, sowing despair and fear in the hearts of his foes.

Tecún Umám was surrounded by his personal escorts, commanded by the captain of the imperial guard, Chilam Kinich, who was fighting with great valor, protecting his lord, making sure he was not felled by one of the Spaniards' long swords or attacked by the dreadful mastiffs. His eyes were constantly scanning the battlefield, alert, poised, killing any enemy that threatened the flank of Tecúm.

In another sector of the battleground, Kakupatak, the war chief, was also dispensing death to his enemies, encouraging his young troops, dispatching many K'akchiquels in his path. He was gratified that his troops, despite their youth, had not abandoned discipline. They were holding their perimeter.

The river was getting more crimson, especially in the areas where the current was decreased by the piled-up cadavers.

Alvarado was beyond himself, swearing constantly, berating his Indian allies, coaxing them to attack, ordering his soldiers to close ranks to avoid defeat. The state of his troops was getting desperate. His agile mind kept playing scenarios, mentally rearranging his forces, trying to make order of the chaos his well-orchestrated assault had become. Like a master chess player, he constantly moved his forces to block advances from his opponent, reinforcing the weak spots. The battlefield was littered with thousands of corpses, sometimes forcing the aggressors to jump over them to avoid getting mired in the fluids draining from the wounded or the recently deceased.

The vacant eyes of the dead were witnesses of the vast carnage piling up during the assault. So many fallen! Young, brave, inexperienced, loyal.

The zopilotes kept watching, circling above, patiently waiting the time to descend and gorge in the feast that for sure was coming.

The frenzy of the *tuns* had reached a crescendo, inciting the troops to hold their positions, to keep the fight, their sound punctuated by the hoarse voices of the defenders shouting orders to their troops to resist the attack.

The air was stale as if sucked out by the powder belched by the cannons and the harquebuses.

The grass of the valley was scorched by the cannons, dead for many years to come, soiled with the blood of the innocent, like lambs being slaughtered by the regiments attacking them.

Chapter 49

"The Spaniards are wavering," Tecún Umám, the Nima Rajpop Achij, the great captain of the K'iche army, shouted over the noise to his war chief, Kakupatak. He continued, "Let's keep up the pressure of our attack. I will lead the charge from the center and you, Tata, will command the right flank. We will move in a pincer movement, squeezing them until they are completely surrounded, and then, we will crush the white barbarians and their lap dogs, the K'akchiquels and the Tz'utujils."

Kakupatak responded affirmatively and started moving with his troops to execute his part of the plan.

On seeing these displacements, Alvarado, more experienced and cunning, guessed the trap. He immediately ordered Olid and Portocarrero to pretend they were retreating. Alvarado's purpose was to lure Tecún's troops away from the heavily defended parapets and then pounce back. He was vowing vociferously to claim revenge for the earlier humiliation of a near defeat! This was his opportunity to wrestle victory from the clutches of defeat.

The feigned withdrawal started in an orderly, measured way, the troops of the foreigners staying close, each soldier protecting his assigned area. They fell back slowly, meter by meter, enticing the K'iche soldiers to pursue them, abandoning their relatively secure positions. The K'iche warriors fell for the trap, more than happy to follow the enemy. They could smell that victory was within their grasp.

The horsemen, relentlessly guiding their horses with great skill, were closing the trap, slowly encircling the unsuspecting K'iche troops, choking them, robbing the pursuers little by little of vital space to maneuver and use their deadly slingshots. Their displacement was hampered even more by the dead bodies, the gore, the discarded equipment, forcing the K'iche warriors to trip one against the other, losing their footing, unable to even use their obsidian-studded clubs. Intoxicated by the prospect of an easy triumph, the squadron leaders of the K'iche urged their troops to pursue the enemy. Soon they found that they were no match for the seasoned Spaniard veterans. The K'iche soldiers had fallen for an old trick.

The Spaniards kept enticing their enemy to follow them. Soon, too soon, dozens of farmer-soldiers, abandoning the discipline that until that moment had maintained, and contrary to urgings from their officers, started to go after supposedly easy picks, breaking ranks, thinking that the enemy was on the run. In their eagerness to claim success, the warriors were reverting to their traditional, disorganized way of fighting openly, man to man. All semblance of order was lost.

The more disciplined Spaniards saw their chance and commenced the counterattack, orderly, methodically, disciplined. Their cannons and harquebuses mowing people left and right, like scythes mowing wheat, the horses trampling with their powerful hooves dozens of terrified fighters.

The mastiffs added to the confusion, ripping apart the hapless soldiers, crunching many with their strong jaws and heavy paws.

Many K'iche warriors had never in their lives seen such powerful horses or those heavy dogs. The hounds were in frenzy, spurred by the smell of blood of the men they were practically devouring, maiming, weakening dozens of able fighters.

Since the K'iche soldiers were carrying *pitos*. Involuntarily many started to blow on them adding more noise to the already loud arena. The sounds of the *pitos* made the mastiffs even more ferocious, wilder, and were now attacking the defenders with savage rage, whimpering, howling and trying to shake loose the noise hurting their ears.

Pretty soon the charging K'iche troops were running for their lives, in their haste to escape abandoning their weapons, searching for sanctuary against the horses and the dogs. The river became their objective, the beacon of salvation, many forgetting they could not swim or that the river in the sector they were attempting to wade was really deep and wide. Many hundreds drowned, with few reaching the safety of their lines across the waters now turned red with the copious amounts of blood flowing from the wounded or dead combatants, spilling into the river.

What initially seemed to be an easy victory for the K'iche was now a rout, like turkey hunting. In their quest for vengeance they had squandered a certain victory.

The blood freely flowing to the river was such that the water pooled by the hundreds of corpses became red, deep crimson. Many years later, the river would be renamed Xequijel, the river of blood or the red river.

The struggle continued for many more hours, the carnage kept mounting, the K'akchiquel and Tz'utujil soldiers exacting a cruel revenge on their former enemies, their ancient brothers.

All was lost. Many heroic K'iche soldiers still kept fighting, making their enemies to pay a heavy price for each palm of ground grabbed.

The stench of the battlefield was becoming overpowering, many fighters retching, unable to control their revulsion.

The Spaniards were urging their allies with imprecations, shouts, sometimes physically pushing them, ordering to butcher their brethren. They wanted to make sure no K'iche survived. The Spaniard soldiers were anxious to get to the palaces and pillage their innards. They were thirsty for gold and riches, which finally was almost within their reach.

Chapter 50

*P*edro de Alvarado saw his chance for redemption, for victory, and kept the pressure, relentlessly advancing, like an avenging angel, possessed, killing or wounding dozens of warriors with his huge sword, by now drenched with blood, his breastplate stained with entrails, his helmet askew, his golden hair matted with sweat, his beard itching with the salt of his perspiration.

Without knowing, Tecún Umán was moving in the same direction as Alvarado. He was getting near him, closer until he could see the blond man riding his mare, dispensing death, pain, and misery like an avenging demon escaped from hell.

Alvarado, unsuspecting his enemy's proximity continued pressing his attack, spurring his mount, trampling many in his path.

When Tecún realized that his nemesis was within his reach, he got nearer, almost to the point of seeing Alvarado's face. Tecún could almost feel the malevolent presence, which made his blood boil, his temper heightened by the chance to avenge the death of many of his soldiers. On realizing this, Tecún advanced with great stealth, as if he was hunting deer, eager to kill, to finish the loathed enemy, the invader of his land.

Tecún still had his long lance and silently thrust it upward, the tip penetrating the chest of the noble mare with a sickening, suckling sound. When the horse felt the piercing stab, his forelegs buckled unseating her rider, who fell to the ground, unbalanced, trying to stand and attempting to gather his sword, afraid of the unknown warrior facing him.

Tecún Umán was poised with his obsidian-studded club, ready to deliver the final blow to his enemy, the hated Spaniard called Tonatiuh by the Tlaxcalans. Unexpectedly, the Nima Rajpop Achij, Tecún Umán, felt his back pierced by a sharp pike wielded by Juan Argueta, the drifter sergeant that had faithfully been shadowing his master, Captain Alvarado. The wound in the chest of Tecún Umán was a large jagged gash that started bleeding copiously, like the waters of the river. The life of Tecún fast ebbing between his fingers, his mouth filled with a pink froth, his breathing short and raspy. Tecún was in shock, rapidly losing consciousness. In his last moments of lucidity, he saw the face of Ixchel, his beloved bride. He felt sad that he had failed her and now his nation would be open to the invader. His life was fading fast, like the sands of an hour clock until he finally collapsed to the ground, inert, lifeless.

Shortly, his *nahual*, the resplendent quetzal, which had been flying overhead descended, landing on the chest of his protégé, as if trying to protect him with his body. On contact with the corpse of his lord, the feathers of the sacred bird were soon soaked with the blood of Tecún, he too slowly dying alongside his master, the Nima Rajpop Achij, Tecún Umam.

Tecún died content that he had given a great battle to the invader Alvarado and his minions, the K'akchiquels and the Tz'utujils almost defeating him and his armies. A great man's life was snuffed, like a candle extinguished by the wind, lost forever.

A dark cloud of quetzals obscured the sun, blocking the light from the face of the fallen hero.

The last Maya prince, Tecún Umán, had succumbed at the hands of that obscure Spaniard soldier, Juan Argueta.

With the death of Tecún Umán, the fate of the K'iche kingdom and his people was sealed.

His nation was no more. It would be buried in the sands of oblivion for many centuries.

Nima Rajpop Achij, Tecún Umám, born Ahau Galel, the last Maya Prince was dead, defending his land against the tidal wave of the Spanish aggressors.

Thus, Tecún Umán was born into the history of his brave nation.

His tomb is unknown; his legacy immortal.

Epilogue

*I*n the following months, with a zeal never seen before, maybe borne from spite, the enduring Maya culture would be erased from the face of the earth, lost to the world for hundreds of years. There would be no more prophesies by the priests. The incredible advances in mathematics and astronomy would also vanish into the darkness of the inquisition, lost to the world for almost five centuries. Many of the splendid Maya temples will be razed; the stones would be used to build the new churches of the Spaniards, consecrated to their God.

Their books and documents would be burned or destroyed by fanatical, ignorant priests and soldiers of fortune.

Tecún's people would be enslaved for many centuries by the conqueror Pedro de Alvarado y Contreras and his army of ragtag

Alvarado had visited on the last Maya a reign of terror with little equivalent in history, fueled mostly by greed, avarice and thirst for glory.

Author's Note

History, though fascinating, is most of the times, an imprecise discipline subject to changes and revisions as time passes by.

With the explosion of knowledge, many facts that once were considered gospel have been reviewed and changed to reflect a more accurate portrayal of the events of that epoch.

The conquest of Guatemala is a brief chapter in the history of the world, a mere blip in the conscience of many nations.

Ahau Galel, the Guatemalan national hero, is better known as Tecún Umán. In the novel, he is also referred as Tekún Umám, Tecún Umán. He was born Ahau Galel from the house of Tekún, the regent family of the K'iche kingdom at the time of the conquest.

Tecún later became the Nima Rajpop Achij, great captain general, grandson of the K'iche king Don K'iqab and would from then on, be addressed as Tecún Umám.

He valiantly opposed the forces commanded by Pedro de Alvarado, native of Badajóz, Spain, who enlisted the aid of the K'akchiquels and the Tz'utujils in his quest to conquer the K'iche. Alvarado also brought with him Tlaxcala and Choluteca indians from the region around Oaxaca.

At the time of the conquest, the Maya were a fragmented nation with the K'iche (Quiché) being the main group.

In writing this book, I attempted to present the human side of Tecún Umán, as well as that of Pedro de Alvarado and his friends and aides, Captain Pedro Portocarrero and Captain Cristobal Olid (de Olid).

Crucial characters of the book are the following:

Doña Luisa de Xicotencalt. She was also called Luisa De Tlaxcala. Was born a princess, daughter of Xicotenga, cacique of the Tlaxcala, whose kingdom was situated in now southern Mexico. Doña Luisa continued at the side of Pedro de Alvarado and eventually married him. From this union, she bore three children, Maria Leonor De Alvarado, Pedro De

Alvarado(Pedrito) and Diego De Alvarado. Later On, Maria Leonor Married Pedro Portocarrero. Pedrito, Maria Leonor and Diego became a new breed of people now called *mestizos*, the result of Spaniard and Indian blood. She moved to the first capital of Guatemala, founded by Alvarado. On her death at a relatively young age, causes unknown, she was buried in the cathedral of the new city. Pedrito, according to historical records, drowned when the ship carrying him floundered in its crossing the Atlantic. Diego De Alvarado Died In Peru @ 1554.

The priests Juan Diaz and Juan Godinez did indeed accompany Alvarado and were instrumental in the polishing of Alvarado's learning.

Recent discoveries had shed light on the way Alvarado almost lost his life at the hands of Tecún Umán but was luckily saved by Argueta, a drifter soldier of fortune that changed the outcome of the final battle between the K'iche and the invading forces of Alvarado. I could not find if his real name was Juan but decided to use it since Juan is a common name in Spain and Latin America.

The notion that Tecún didn't know the difference between the horse and Alvarado was dispelled. The Maya believed in the *nahual*, a guardian angel-like, Tecún was fully aware that beast and master were altogether different.

The caciques Xahil and Acajal certainly existed and were the chieftains of the K'akchiquel (Cachiquels) and Tz'utujil kingdoms, both of which were sworn enemies of the K'iche and fought constantly against them.

Don K'iqab was the grandfather of Tecún and perished in one of the many battles against the K'akchiquels and the Tz'utujils.

The *zanjas* trenches were actually excavated by *zappers* as described in the book, with some twists to accommodate the story. The K'iche also used guerilla warfare against the aggressors. This and other facts are described in a study done by the Guatemalan army, published in 1963, entitled *La Muerte de Tecún Umán* [The Death of Tecún Umán].

The mastiffs were there, and there is a painting in the palace of the captains, in Antigua Guatemala, Guatemala, that portrays Alvarado and a huge dog sitting by his side.

Another book that proved invaluable was *Historia de Guatemala* written by Francis Polo Sifontes, published by Editorial Evergraficas SA, Spain.

I got some ideas, especially in regard to Alvarado's early life and his meeting the gypsies from an excellent novel entitled *The Brave Dogs*, written by Kenny Fitzgerald.

Ixchel, her mother Ixmucané, and Tecún's friends Ixpiyacoc and Vukub are mythological figures from the Popol Vuh.

K'etzalin is the creation of my imagination.

Kakupatak is the Maya god of war.

The brothers of Alvarado, his parents, as well as his cousin Rodrigo were real people, and some came with him to the New World.

Hernán Cortés was Alvarado's superior and they fought together during the battles against the Aztecs. Cortés later was named governor of New Spain and finally *Virrey* (viceroy).

Other excellent references were: Anales de los Cachiqueles. *Titulo K'oyoi. Titulo De Los Señores de Totonicapán* by anonymous authors.

The city of K'umarkaj or Q'umarkaj was later known as Santa Cruz del Quiché and can be visited in the Department of el Quiché, in northern Guatemala.

The capital of the K'akchiquels was called Iximche. It still is known as it was before and is situated close to the town of Tecpán, in the highlands of Guatemala. The ruins are also called Utatlán.

The name of the capital of the Tz'utujils was lost to posterity or was not important enough to merit a footnote in history, but it was situated near the shores of Lake Atitlán. Most recently it was confirmed that the metropolis was called Chuitinamit, now Santiago Atitlán.

The battles, troops' disposition, and logistics are part real and part fiction to accommodate the flow of the story.

The escape of the women, children and elders to Zaculeu is fictional, though is something that could have happened.

I hope you have enjoyed this novel.

This book is also available in Spanish.

In preparation the final saga of the conquest of Guatemala, tentatively entitled:

The Eclipse of Iximché.

A synopsis of chapter 1 follows:

1527

The child was burning with fever, his little body almost convulsing with the high temperature; the priests attending the child were baffled. They could not find an explanation for the fever, despite the incantations and administrations of potions.

Few days later, the little kid's body was covered with small blisters, reddish, extremely itchy. The child appeared really sick, frightened, his lips parched due to dehydration and his senses almost lost to the ravages of fever.

Few days later the child expired but many more similar cases followed.

It was the first epidemic of small pox in the Americas that almost wiped the whole indian population. The disease happened several years after the first visit of the Spaniards to the capitals of Iximche and Chuitinamit, where they came to negotiate a peace treaty as emissaries of the governor of Oaxaca, Pedro de Alvarado y Contreras, an agreement ratified by Acajal the cacique of the K'akchiquels and Xahil, the head of the Tz'utujils,

Later on, the two chieftains were lamenting their alliance with the Spaniards which had become cruel masters and were subjecting the indians to unusual punishment and hard labor. The seed of rebellion were slowly growing and taking root amongst the two indian nations.

Conrad Samayoa
Orland Park, IL. 2012.

Made in the USA
San Bernardino, CA
27 June 2020